DESERTS, DRIVING, & DERELICTS

A Camper And Criminals Cozy Mystery

Book Two

BY
TONYA KAPPES

TONYA KAPPES
WEEKLY NEWSLETTER

Want a behind-the-scenes journey of me as a writer?
The ups and downs, new deals, book sales, giveaways and more? I share it all! Join the exclusive Southern Sleuths private group today! Go to www.patreon.com/Tonyakappesbooks

As a special thank you for joining, you'll get an exclusive copy of my cross-over short story, *A CHARMING BLEND.* Go to Tonyakappes.com and click on subscribe at the top of the home page.

"Did I interrupt you?" I gazed over at the table.

"No. It's just me." She headed to the door, continuing to blot the napkin on her arm. "Fifi just had her hair clipped, and her nails are so sharp. She scratched me—by accident, of course—when I picked her up."

"Do you want me to look at it?" I asked.

"No. No. I'll be fine. Follow me to Harrison's office. That's where I keep the checks." She walked through the open deck doors. Some stray feathers from her housecoat floated behind her.

"Harrison?" I didn't know who that was.

"My deceased husband." She stopped in her tracks on the way down the hallway. "I guess that's something you and I have in common."

She put her hand on the doorknob of the closed door.

"I guess you checked up on me." I pinched a fake smile, thinking only of a tip.

"Hank told me who you were after you pushed the little cleaning cart around the house this morning." She turned the knob. "I think it's admirable how you're working your way to pay off your husband's mistakes and misdeeds."

"Ex," I said through an exhausted sigh.

She opened the door and took a couple of steps in before she flipped on the light and let out a bloodcurdling scream before fainting.

Camille Braun was sitting behind Harrison's desk in his big leather chair with a knife stuck in her chest, her eyes wide open.

CHAPTER ONE

"Well, well, well."

Someone standing in the sun's rays cast a shadow over my lawn chair. Dottie Swaggert, the manager and social coordinator of Happy Trails, and I had taken a few minutes to enjoy the pleasant early morning warmth by the campground's lake before the heat wave of the Indian summer took over in the afternoon.

The person dropped a knapsack on the ground next to their feet. "If it ain't May-bell-line Grant, then my eyes are deceiving me," he said with a heavy Southern twang.

Lordy. I shielded my eyes from the sun and hoped that it was the hot summer sun playing tricks on my mind. Was it really who I thought it was? I scooted up onto my elbows, blinking a few times to try to get the sunspots to go away so I could see clearly.

"Your eyes are deceiving you." Dottie Swaggert moved the tinfoil-covered piece of cardboard from underneath her chin. She used her fingers to fluff up the curls in her short red hair that'd been flattened from lying down. "Now pick up that backpack, get out of my sun, and get on the trail to Daniel Boone National Forest right through them trees." Dottie pointed to the tree line behind the lake, where many

1

different levels of trails started for the campers of Happy Trails. Every once in a while, we got a stray hiker or two.

Satisfied with herself, Dottie laid her head back down and put the cardboard back up underneath her chin. "Honey, we see all kinds during these Indian summers." She glanced over at me. "You know if I said Indian summer anywhere else than right here, I'd be considered of ill-repute."

My eyes adjusted, and sure enough, it was exactly who I thought it was. Just a little older.

"Go on!" Dottie said with some frustration and flung her hand out.

"Bobby Ray Bond?" I questioned and pushed myself up off the chair.

I stood face-to-face with the very person who gave me the money to leave on that Greyhound bus to New York City twelve years ago.

"Heeeeeere's Bobby!" He held his arms out and put on a funny grin like Jack Nicholson in *The Shining*.

We'd spent many nights watching *The Shining* over and over. Bobby did the best impersonation of Jack Nicholson, down to the crazy eyes.

"Bobby!" I squealed and threw my arms around him. It didn't take long for my nose to catch on to his bad body odor. I took a step back. With my hands on my hips and a smile on my face, I asked, "What on earth are you doing here?"

Bobby Ray had on a pair of dirty jeans and a filthy white T-shirt with the neck stretched out. He had brown eyes that used to match his head full of brown hair, but time seemed to have taken that away from him, leaving him a thin comb-over.

"I came to see my one true May-bell-ine." He winked. "Look at you. All grown up and stuff. Running a campground. Back in Kentucky. Then I went and Googled you down at the community center. Literally almost fainted when I seen all the hashtags with your name. I told everyone that my May-bell-ine had hit it big time, owning her own campground and all."

"Dottie, this is Bobby Ray Bond. Bobby and I were in the same foster family. He was the only one with a good job, and he gave me enough money to not only get a Greyhound bus ticket out of Kentucky, but also the initial payment for flight attendant school."

Then it hit me like the stink his body was emitting. It was time to pay the piper, and Bobby Ray just so happened to be the one tooting the horn.

"How did you find me?" I asked leerily.

"You could've knocked my teeth out when I saw your interview in *National Parks of America* magazine. I said to myself, Bobby Ray, is that our May-bell-ine Grant? I responded to myself, Nah. Our May-bell-ine would've called if she was in Kentucky because that's what she said in the middle of the night before she left."

My mouth dried and I gulped. It wasn't that I didn't want to call him, but it was a part of my life that I wanted to forget.

"The more I read it, the more I couldn't believe my eyes. As sure as Shinola, it was my May-bell-ine Grant, who's not only grown up but has a campground of her very own." He grinned. "Looky at you."

"And look at you." There was some apparent sarcasm in Dottie's response. "You ought to be ashamed of yourself," she said with a little fire behind her words. She stood up. Her temper was flaring up as bright as her hair. "You comin' here and tryin' to mooch off Mae West now that she's made a name for herself."

Bobby Ray jumped.

"Woman! What's wrong with you?" he protested. "Bobby Ray Bond doesn't mooch off no one. Especially not May-bell-ine." His face scrunched up in disapproval of Dottie's accusations.

"Don't you be callin' me 'woman'!" She jabbed some uppercuts with her hands fisted. I'm sure she'd learned those in the Strike Jazzercise class she'd been taking with Queenie French, one of our friends. "Now, you get on out of here like I told you to earlier."

"Hold on." I positioned myself between them, arms outstretched. "Dottie," I said, putting my arms down, straightening my shoulders, and choking out the next words. "If it weren't for Bobby Ray, I'd not be right where I'm standing."

"Mmmhhhh," Bobby agreed. "She's right. Right as rain."

I gulped back what felt like tears coming up, stinging my nose. What Bobby had done for me so many years ago was a blessing, and it made me cry then, much like it was doing now.

"I just can't believe it's you." I wiped a tear from my cheek. He smiled. "I guess I need to stop blubbering and get to work. But I'll get you settled first," I said to Bobby and glanced over at Dottie. She was still glaring at Bobby Ray. "Dottie, I'll meet you in the office in a few minutes. We can get the final details worked out for the Summer Sizzler."

"You mean you ain't had that Summer Sizzler party I read about in the magazine?" Bobby bounced on the souls of his filthy shoes. "I love me a good party."

"You're staying?" Well, crap. Now I couldn't help but wonder if Dottie was right about him coming here for something more than just a short visit.

"Yes, I am." He rocked back and forth. "A few days anyways."

"Bet he hangs around longer," Dottie muttered under her breath as she headed off in the direction of the office at the entrance of the campground.

"Bobby, would you like a drink?" I asked, gesturing for him to follow me to my camper. "I've got some homemade sweet tea that's been soaking in the sun since yesterday. I'm figuring that it's probably about ready."

"You're speaking my language, May-bell-ine." He hurried behind me.

"I don't go by Maybelline anymore. When I moved to NYC, I shortened it to Mae," I said.

It wasn't because I was trying to escape the name from my past; it was because my mama truly named me after the beauty product. I was so tired of the jokes that came with it. New York was a fresh start, and it was Bobby Ray who I had to thank. Since I'd been back in Kentucky, I'd wondered over several occasions what my life would look like if I'd not left twelve years ago. It was no good trying to figure out the what ifs, so I'd forced my thoughts to something different, like what Ty Randal was doing back in San Francisco.

On our way to my camper, I couldn't help but look at Ty Randal's camper. Was he ever going to come back now that his father had recovered and he didn't have to live in Normal to look after his siblings?

"You sure have a nice place here." Bobby brought me out of my thoughts.

"It wasn't like this at all when I first got here," I said, getting a whiff of Bobby's odor on the downwind, which was probably the only breeze we'd have all day. It was going to be a scorcher.

That was Kentucky weather. It was like Mother Nature had a plan, but Father Time was driving and didn't ask for directions. The seasons were all over the place. But it was also one of the things I did miss about Kentucky while I was away—the different seasons and the beauty each one brought to the area.

"The lake was a mess, and there wasn't any grass." I continued to tell him about how I'd taken possession of the campground that was one day away from being shut down by the National Park Service. "I'm sure you know that my ex-husband was Paul West."

I took the flamingo key chain out of the pocket of my shorts and unlocked the camper door. I grabbed the jug of sweet sun tea that I'd put on the picnic table outside of my camper yesterday. The color was nice and orange. Perfect.

"I wasn't going to bring it up, but now that you have…" Bobby took the couple of steps up into the camper. "I did read about it when I Googled you. Mostly, I was hurt that you didn't invite me to the wedding."

"I wish I wasn't invited either." I half joked. "But the good thing is I'm back in Kentucky and really enjoying life now." I turned around inside of the camper and reached out to touch his arm. "I'm so glad you are here. Now, it looks like you've had a long day already."

"Do I look that bad?" He brushed his hands down his dirty clothes. "I walked here."

"You're kidding me?" My jaw practically dropped to the floor. No wonder his shoes were torn up and his clothes were dirty. "That had to take days."

"Yep, but you're worth it, May-bel…" He paused. "Mae."

"I'll get you a big glass filled with iced tea while you grab a shower in my bathroom right back there." I gestured to the back of the camper and grabbed a plastic glass to get his tea fixed.

"Are you sure?" he asked.

"Of course. I hope you stay with me while you're here." I knew that I was going to regret that as soon as it came out of my mouth.

"I was hoping you'd say that." That put a big grin on his face. "I'll be right out."

"Take your time. I'm actually going to run up to my storage unit. I think I've got some men's clothes in there." I went back to the door. "You'll find everything you need under the sink."

He'd already disappeared into the bathroom before I could finish my sentence. Over the past couple of months, I'd invested in a used golf cart to help get around the campground. Mostly, my handyman, Henry, used it.

It was perfect for a situation like this. Instead of walking down to the storage unit to grab some old clothes of Paul's for Bobby, I could jump in and drive it up to the storage unit, get the clothes, and be back before he finished showering.

Some of my stuff from my previous life was stored in boxes in one of the storage units. Most of the boxes were fancy clothes that I'd yet to sell on eBay. Setting up an eBay shop was another awesome thing Abby Fawn had done initially to raise money for the campground. I wasn't going to be using high heels and sequin dresses around here, so we sold them on eBay for a crazy price and used the money to help fix the washers and dryers.

I'd still not gone through all the other boxes that contained knick-knacks. If I hadn't missed them by now, I probably never would. Eventually, I'd go through them. It just wasn't high on my priority list.

Last time I was in there, I had seen a box labeled "Paul's Clothes". It would be good enough for Bobby to wear until I could get downtown and pick up some clothes from the secondhand store for him. I needed to go downtown anyway.

The storage units were situated slightly behind the office, covered by big oak trees. There were ten standard metal units. We had a few campers who paid a yearly lot fee, but only stayed in their campers for a couple of weeks or months each year for vacation. Those residents were the ones who usually rented a storage unit for their golf carts or other things they didn't want to store in their campers.

I put the key into the lock and twisted it until I heard a click. The doors were like a garage door that lifted up. I bent down and lifted it until I heard it lock in place at the top so the thing wouldn't fall down on me. I'd learned my lesson the hard way.

Paul's box was in the back-left corner. I dragged it to the front of the unit.

Anger swelled up inside of me when I got a whiff of Paul's cologne. I'd know that smell anywhere. Gucci for Men. I dug through the box until I reached a couple of short-sleeved shirts. It was hot as Haiti here, and long sleeves would roast Bobby Ray like a s'more.

"You gonna let him stay here?" Dottie caught me off guard. I looked back at her standing in the doorway of the unit, a cigarette stuck in the corner of her lip. "He's here to use you."

"You scared me." I held a polo shirt up to my chest to see if it would fit Bobby. "Yes. I'm going to let him stay here with me. He's not here to use me."

"Mae, I'm telling you. I've seen his kind before. He's like a bugger on your finger, you won't be able to thump him off," she said, warning me in a way only she'd be able to.

"He's only passing through." Well, technically he didn't say that, but it was good enough to get Dottie off my back until I did figure out just how long he was staying. "I do owe him."

"Then give him the money back." She took the cig out of her mouth and pointed her finger at me. "How much did he give you?" she asked.

"It was about three thousand dollars." I went back to the box and dug deeper until I found a pair of khaki pants. I held them up in the air. "These will do until I can get some shorts at the secondhand store." I draped them over my arm.

"I'm telling you," she said when I walked by her to leave the storage unit, "he's got more guts than you can hang on a fence showing up here like that."

"Wait." I stopped and motioned her to come out so I could close the storage door. "I thought it was commonplace to just show up unannounced around here."

"Only when you don't want a favor," she spat. "Good news, we had four more calls about the one cancellation. Shoooweee." She pulled a napkin from her bra and wiped her brow before dabbing her chest with it and putting it back. "It's gonna be a killer."

"I'll see you later." I closed the box back up and decided to leave it where it was. The garage door wheels squealed when I pulled it back down and locked it. I got into the golf cart and took off, waving my hand in the air, leaving Dottie standing there with a sassy look on her face.

Bobby Ray was whistling in the shower when I got back to the camper. It brought back so many memories. You always knew where Bobby was because he always whistled a tune. His happy-go-lucky attitude was the one thing that made me love being around him so much. It made me happy to see he'd not changed all that much.

No matter what my gut told me, I was going to be nice and kind to Bobby. He deserved that.

Before he finished with his lengthy shower, I unlocked the glove box in my RV and got into my little stash of cash. It was the only thing that Paul had done right by me before the FBI seized everything and hauled him off to jail. He'd left me one hundred thousand dollars in a secret sock drawer in our Manhattan apartment. I'd used some here and there, mainly to pay back what Paul had taken from Dottie, so there wasn't a lot left, but I couldn't forget what Dottie had suggested about paying Bobby back. In business, there were never handouts. Bobby walking halfway across the state to find me made me suspicious. It was best just to head it off at the pass.

I hurried up and counted out three thousand dollars after I heard the water turn off.

"Bobby"—I knocked on the door of the bathroom—"I've got some extra clothes for you on the floor outside the door." I put them down on the ground and walked back to the kitchen area of the camper, which was about five steps away, busying myself with the tea.

In no time, Bobby was standing next to me, smelling much better.

"I'll take your clothes to the laundromat when I go to town later. I also need to go to the Tough Nickel Thrift Shop. I can pick you up a couple of outfits while I'm there." I handed him a glass of fresh sweet tea. Then I tugged the cash out of my back pocket. "I'm so glad you are here. Now I don't have to hunt you down to repay you."

His eyes rounded as he fixed them on the wad of cash.

"It's all three thousand I owe you." I handed it to him.

"With interest?" he asked. When I looked at him, he smiled. "Just kiddin'." He took a drink of tea and put the cash in the front pocket of Paul's khakis. "Mae, I'm not here to collect this money."

He wasn't fooling me because he wasn't digging it back out of his pocket.

"I gave that money to you, but I can't say it's not come at a time when I'm down on my luck." This surprised me because Bobby was such a good mechanic. He always held down some sort of mechanic job and a side gig at the local fast-food chain when we were kids. "All these fancy cars and technology changing like it's done has really put a dent in what I know."

"I've never thought about mechanics and new technology," I said.

"I'm not used to these fancy clothes." He wiped his hands down his chest. He was avoiding eye contact with me. Knowing Bobby Ray like I did, he was embarrassed at where his life had led him.

"You can have them." I patted his back.

"This sure is a fancy camper." He looked around. "I don't think I've ever seen walls like this."

"Let me show you what it used to look like." I took my phone off the charger and clicked onto the photos app. I swiped the screen until I found them. "As you can see, it wasn't that great. But I've learned a lot since living here. I've got some great friends that can decorate on a budget. These walls are old wood pallets that I've turned into that popular shiplap."

I'd used every bit of space possible. I'd taken down all the walls and made it an open concept plan with the kitchen and family room in one big room. We'd put up shiplap walls painted white. I'd gotten a cute café table with two chairs from the Tough Nickel, as well as a small leather couch. It was perfect for one. The floors were redone with a prefabricated gray wood. The kitchen cabinets and all the storage cabinets were white. I'd transformed the little camper into a country farmhouse.

I'd strung twinkle lights everywhere I could. The bathroom was redone with a tile shower and upgraded toilet. Then I had my bedroom in the back. I'd opted to buy a new mattress and used some nailed together wooden pallets I'd painted pink as a headboard. I'd gotten a dresser with four drawers from the Tough Nickel that went perfect with my distressed look. The twinkle lights added a bit of romance, along with the fuzzy rugs and milk glass vases full of fresh flowers or wildflowers that grew here in the Daniel Boone National Forest.

"By the look of it, life's agreeing with you." He sat down in one of the chairs at the table.

"You know, it's hard to even remember how a few months ago, I was actively trying to find a buyer so I could go back to being a flight attendant." I sat down across from him. "Now, I couldn't imagine not living here."

"Even after they found your husband in that lake?" he asked.

"Ex." I took a drink of my tea. Without bragging, I'd really outdone myself on this tea. I was getting better and better at making it taste good. "Nope. I took the negative and turned that around. Enough about me, tell me about you. Where are you headed?"

"Why, I'm here." He patted the kitchen table.

"Here? As in Normal?" I tried to dance around the big elephant in the room.

"Yep. I figured you'd need someone lookin' after you like I used to do. That's why I decided to head here." He patted the table again.

"Oh, no." I waved off his ridiculous notion. "You don't need to do that. I'm just fine. But I sure have enjoyed our little visit, and I'm glad I got to pay you back. Where are you staying?"

"You don't have any open campers?" he asked. He'd obviously done more than just look me up. He looked up the entire Happy Trails website. "I seen where you have some campers for rent."

As much as I wanted to say they were all taken and get him out of my life, because he was here for something, I couldn't let him just loiter around Normal.

"Actually, they are little bungalows, but of course you can stay in one. I have to check with Dottie to see which one is open." There was a smile on my face, but my stomach churned. For a brief second, I felt like I was going to throw up. But why?

CHAPTER TWO

"Thank you for coming in." Alison Gilbert, the young reporter from *National Parks of America* magazine, greeted me all bright-eyed and bushy-tailed. She wore black sandals and a midcalf-length red dress with small black polka dots. Her brown hair was cut to her chin. "We are so glad you agreed to the interview. Follow me."

She hurried down the hall at the Daniel Boone National Forest office, talking over her shoulder and guiding me to the room where she was going to perform the interview. She set her bag on the long conference table.

"Now, we can relax." She turned slightly to look at me as she continued to walk down the hall. "I have coffee here, along with some donuts. Please, help yourself."

I walked over to the coffee bar, catching my reflection in the glass window that overlooked a beautiful area of the national park, and noticed my hair had doubled in size on the ride over to the office. That was the problem with curly hair and humidity. The two didn't play nice with each other.

"Thank you," I said and pulled a handful of hair over my shoulder to one side. "Would you like a cup too?" I asked and poured a cup of coffee.

"That'd be great." Her hand was buried in her bag. She dug around for a few more minutes, finally pulling out a camera.

"You do remember the terms I agreed to?" I wanted to confirm before we got started.

"Yep." Her head slowly nodded. She fiddled with her phone and sat it down on the table. "No particulars about your husband or the Ponzi scheme, but you're okay with talking about how you acquired Happy Trails Campground, bringing more tourists to Normal during a slow economic time."

"Ex-husband," I muttered, heading over to the table, setting a cup of coffee in front of her, and then walking over to look at the donuts.

"Right." She pulled in a deep breath. "I'm going to tape it on my phone, if that's okay," she said. "I like to go back and listen to the interview while I'm writing the piece. I want to make sure I don't leave anything out."

"Sure." I grabbed one of the glazed donuts and took a modest bite. If I were alone in my camper, I'd just stuff my face with all of it and lick my fingers after.

"Interview with Mae West, owner of Happy Trails Campground located deep in the Daniel Boone National Forest in Normal, Kentucky." She smiled. "Normal," she repeated, laughing. The tone of her voice had changed into a very professional one. "There's really nothing that's been normal in Happy Trails for many years."

I didn't know what she wanted me to say, so I just took a sip of coffee.

"How did you acquire Happy Trails?" she asked.

"It's no secret that I was married to Paul West." If whoever reads this article in *National Parks of America* magazine hadn't heard of my ex-husband, then they'd literally been living off the land in one of these parks with their head stuck under a rock. "Years ago, during his college years, he got possession of the campground." I left out the part where he'd actually made a bet with the original owner, Ron Randal, who now owned the Normal Diner. Ron had made a bet with the young go-getter. Paul was never one to turn down a bet, even when he thought he might lose. In this case, he won. And here I was today. "Years later, he gave me the campground."

"Gave it to you?" she asked.

"After Paul went to jail, all of my possessions were seized, except for Happy Trails Campground and the camper I live in because they were in my name only." There wasn't any sense in reliving the entire story of how my lawyer had broken the bad news to me in his Manhattan office, trading my luxury car keys for a flamingo key chain with a camper key dangling off it.

I had no idea Paul had owned a campground. It was a shock to me how, years before, he'd deeded the property over to me. Just one of many things I didn't know. In fact, I didn't even know my husband like I thought I did.

"After I found out that I owned Happy Trails, I made a visit and haven't left. I fell completely in love with camping life and the camp-ground itself." I left out all the in-between stuff like the shock of my new life and living arrangements. Something I was embarrassed about now, but it truly had been a scary time for me.

"You're being modest." Alison scooted up in the chair and rested her forearms on the edge of the conference table. "I want to get to the nitty-gritty. I've talked to a few Happy Trails residents who have made the campground their year-round home. They tell me that Happy Trails was almost inhabitable. After I did a little digging into your married life, I have to assume it was hard for you to go from a mansion in the Hamptons to a tiny camper."

"I admit I was taken aback when I pulled into Happy Trails the first time. The Kentucky bluegrass had been burnt up, the lake had a mucky film over it, and the buildings were in bad shape." There was no denying that Happy Trails had come a long way since I moved to Normal a few months ago. "I'm happy to say that it's fully back up on its feet and we are booked for the next three seasons."

"That's fascinating. I mean, you waltz into Normal as this hoity-toity New York City housewife with all the luxuries the world could offer. You walked into a crazy situation where almost all the residents of Happy Trails had been victims of your husband."

"Ex, and I didn't waltz." My eyes narrowed as I wondered where this interview was going.

She grazed over my comment and continued to look down at her notes.

"I mean, he didn't pay the manager for years, though he did let her live there for free. It was run-down and nothing worked, including the laundry machines. Your husband swindled a lot of Normal residents out of their retirement accounts. How did it feel to be the most hated woman in the town?" She smiled. Her words were like daggers.

"Well, you've done quite a lot of research." I could've reminded her that I didn't really want to talk about what Paul had done to the people of Normal, but I decided to deal with it head-on. Seriously, how many people were reading *National Parks of America* magazine? "I'm fully aware of what Paul did to the people and the town of Normal. Especially when a big chunk of their economy comes from the campground. So, when I saw what a disarray Happy Trails was in, I decided it was time to make things right with the entire community."

"That's when you came up with the brilliant social media campaign?" She was finally getting to the true reason for the interview.

"I have to give credit to my friend Abby Fawn. She's the librarian at the Normal County Library. As you pointed out, the laundry machines at Happy Trails weren't working, and having driven from New York, I needed to do laundry." The memory of my meeting the ladies of the Laundry Club was very fond. I loved telling the story. "I took my laundry to the Laundry Club."

"The Laundry Club is a full-service laundromat located in downtown Normal. Correct?" she asked.

"Yes. Though it's so much more than that. There's fresh coffee, jigsaw puzzles, a book club. It's like a community." I couldn't stop my smile from growing. "That's where I met a group of women I consider my friends. It's like meeting your friends at a coffee shop, only it's a laundromat."

"Tell me about the women." She seemed to be really interested.

"First, there's Dottie Swaggert, then Queenie French, Abby Fawn, and Betts Hager." Even though I was telling the story to her phone, Alison was still taking notes. "They welcomed me with open arms and really took me under their wing. Abby is the one who took my idea about having some sort of fundraiser to help bring the campground back to what it used to be in its glory days and ran with it. She did all the social media hashtagging, and it just took off."

"That's what brings us here today. There was so much buzz about the grand reopening of Happy Trails that you ended up booking all the lots for the next year. No one even seemed to care that your husband's body floated to the top of the lake. Wasn't he murdered?"

She had to add in that last part, didn't she? I lowered my eyes and stared at her for a second. She fidgeted a smidgen as if she realized she was teetering on a fine line.

"Ex," I sighed, grabbing another donut. This time, I stuffed it in my mouth just as I heard the camera click. "You aren't going to print that one, are you?"

"You're originally from Kentucky." She'd obviously been digging around more than just my married life. My palms started to sweat and itch. "Why don't you tell me about that?"

"There's really nothing to tell. It was a lifetime ago." I pinched a smile. "I'm happy to say that I'm back in Kentucky and enjoying living at Happy Trails Campground. We are ready for more families to join us for a terrific vacation." I spouted off the office phone number and the website URL, which was also Abby's doing. "We have a monthly party where we get together for food and friendship. It's free to the public. This month's is about this late Indian summer we are having, so it has a desert theme. Dottie Swaggert is the social coordinator for Happy Trials. If you look on social media, using hashtag Summer Sizzler, you'll find all the information you need. Come one, come all."

"Thank you for taking the time to talk to me today. I know I probably pushed a little too much, but I think everyone is going to love how you completely turned the campground around and brought a feel-good story to Normal, Kentucky." Alison stood up and gathered her belongings. "I ran by the campground earlier and took some photos. I hope you don't mind."

"Not at all." I took another donut. "Please let us know when we are in it so we can frame the article and hang it on the wall in the office."

Little did I realize just how many people did subscribe to *National Parks of America* magazine, but I was soon going to find out.

CHAPTER THREE

I'd gone back to the bedroom to gather my laundry to take to the Laundry Club, and by the time I came back, Bobby Ray had fallen asleep at the kitchen table.

I didn't have the heart to wake him up. After all, he'd walked all the way to Normal and he had to be exhausted. I scribbled a quick note with my cell phone number on it and told him to go to the campground office to use the phone if he needed me, which I didn't anticipate.

The humidity hit me as soon as I opened the door. My hair was growing by the second. The Ford Escort was going to be as hot as a firecracker when I got in.

Betts Hager had played an instrumental part in getting me the Ford Escort to drive around town instead of the camper. The camper was nice to drive when I went to visit other parks, but not to run errands. That would take forever since I'd have to secure everything in the camper that wasn't nailed, screwed, or tied down.

I was truly grateful for the car. The Escort was a donation from the Normal Baptist Church, the church where Betts's husband, Lester, was the pastor.

Grassel's Gas Station was the only gas station in downtown Normal. Joel Grassel was the only employee and mechanic. I'd heard him say over and over that he wished he knew a good mechanic to hire. I just might have the one for him. Stopping by to see him went on my mental list of things I had to do while I was in town.

The trees were in full late summer bloom, and they stood like soldiers on each side of the curvy country road on the way into town, giving a nice shade that sent a cool breeze through the rolled-down windows. Though the campground was considered to be in the country at the base of the Daniel Boone National Forest, it only took a short five to ten minutes, depending on if you got behind a tractor or slow driver, to get into the cozy downtown area. By the time I'd made it to town, my shirt was drenched with sweat.

The heat didn't seem to bother the tourists though. The downtown businesses looked busy with people coming and going. The sidewalks were filled with what looked to be customers window-shopping.

The little shops ranged from the Smelly Dog Groomer to the Laundry Club Laundromat.

Each shop was freestanding with a small courtyard between shops. This allowed each shop to have a unique feature to offer customers.

Deters's Feed-N-Seed had an adorable pop-up tent with a campfire and a s'more-making station for customers. The tented chalkboard sign in front of the Sweet Smell Flower Shop said there was a succulent plant craft in their courtyard. Succulent plants were a perfect touch for an RV and easy to take care of.

Main Street was divided by a median with a one-way street on each side. I circled the median when I noticed a parking space right in front of the Tough Nickel. It was perfect. I'd get Bobby Ray a couple of outfits, head over to the Laundry Club to wash them with the little bit of clothes I had, and stop by to see Joel before I headed back to the campground. It sounded like a good plan.

The median was a combination of grass and stepping-stones that was packed with people walking around or sitting on the picnic tables under the pavilion. There were more picnic tables among the large oak trees on each side of the amphitheater. A few children were running around the open-air theater with their arms out like airplanes.

Normal really did know how to showcase Southern charm. Thick white pillars, like you'd see on the front porch of a plantation home, held up the pavilion. The real gas lanterns hanging from the lampposts added to the charm along with the ceramic planters that showcased the amazing wildflowers that bloomed in the hot heat. Like the campground, twinkle lights were strung all over the place.

"Good afternoon, Mae." Buck, the owner of the Tough Nickel, greeted me from behind the glass counter that was in the middle of the open store. "How's that couch working out for you?"

"I love it. It's the perfect size for me to lie on and relax." I smiled. "I have to admit that sometimes I fall asleep on it and don't move until the next morning."

"When you get older"—he rubbed his neck—"you'll pay for that."

He continued to rub his neck like there was a kink in it. He had coal-black hair and was tall and skinny. From what I'd gathered, he was in his late sixties, but didn't look past his fifties.

"I'm actually here to check out the men's clothes. Size thirty-two shorts and medium tees or short-sleeved shirts." I headed to the steps that led upstairs to where he kept the clothing section of the store.

All the items on the lower level were antiques and not thrift store items. The thrift store section was in the upper level of the building.

"You know where they are." He went back to whatever he was doing.

The steps creaked with every step I took. Heat rose, and in this old-house-turned-shop, the air was thick, almost choking me by the time I got to the top.

Thankfully, the clothes were hung and labeled by size. I just grabbed a couple of tan shorts and some basic shirts. It'd be plenty for Bobby Ray since I still planned to look through Paul's boxes in the storage unit back at the campground.

When I walked back down the steps to pay for the clothes, I noticed Joel Grassel, owner of Grassel's Gas Station, leaning up against the counter talking to Buck. He had on his usual overalls with grease spots. He was a hard worker and it showed.

"I see your car is still running." Joel rubbed the top of his buzz cut with his hand.

"It's perfect. If you get a lead on a pretty cheap car, I'm in the market to buy one and let the church have this one back." I put the armful of clothes on the counter.

Buck picked each one up and used the old cash register to ring me up.

"Actually, I was going to stop by and see you on my way back to Happy Trails. Are you still looking for a mechanic?" I asked.

"Yeah. A good one that can work on farming equipment, campers, and a few cars. You know any?" he asked.

"I do. I have a friend in town, and he's here because he's between jobs." I took the money out of my purse and handed it to Buck after he gave me total. "He said it's really hard to get work because of the technology in new cars."

"That's why I'm having a hard time finding help. No one wants to work on the old engines." Joel shook his head. "Why is it that no one wants to work anymore?"

"Can I send him to the gas station to talk to you?" I asked, taking the bag of clothes Buck put on the counter.

"I'd love to talk to him. And if he's a friend of yours, he's got to be a hard worker." Joel took the greasy hanky from the front pocket of his overalls and wiped his hands. He took a card from his wallet. "Give him this."

"I will." I put the card in my back pocket. "His name is Bobby Ray Bond."

"I look forward to meeting him." He gave me one big nod before he and Buck went back to their conversation.

Instead of moving the car and risking not finding a closer parking spot near the Laundry Club, I got my bag of dirty laundry, added the thrift-shop clothes I'd gotten for Bobby Ray, slung it over my shoulder, and dodged the people on the busy sidewalk.

The Laundry Club was packed too. All the machines were taken.

"If it ain't May-bell-ine Grant." Queenie French smiled as bright as the yellow and teal leggings, matching top, and white legwarmers she was wearing. It was one of her many Jazzercise outfits. She was an instructor and, from what I'd heard, did pretty well for her age.

"Dottie called, huh?" I flipped the laundry bag from my shoulder to the ground, looking around to see if one of the machines was open.

"She couldn't wait to tell us." Queenie adjusted her headband and tapped on the electric globe, where she pretended to see into the future. She couldn't. She just liked to shock people who came into the laundromat. "I see in your future a man from your past that's going to take you to the cleaners. And I don't mean the Laundry Club." She let out a laugh, making everyone in the laundromat turn to see what was so funny.

I'd opted to use the washing machines closest to the front of the shop. With the bag open, I sorted between the whites and the darks.

"Stop it." I laughed. "If it weren't for Bobby Ray, I'd not be here right now. Besides, I paid him back the money he loaned me so there's no miscommunication."

"That's good," Abby Fawn said.

"Hi," I greeted Abby, the Normal librarian and local Tupperware consultant. "I didn't see you over there."

"I'm filling in the bookshelf." Instead of throwing away old and beat-up books, she'd bring them to the Laundry Club. "Now that we have so many tourists, they love reading and the books fly off the shelf."

It was one of those take-what-you-want shelves, and it made Abby's heart soar. Abby took her phone out of her pocket.

"Hashtag new books at the Laundry Club bookshelf. Hashtag laundry. Hashtag Normal." She spoke out loud while she did all of her social media posting. She put her phone back in her pocket after a few more taps. "I just made some fresh coffee too." Abby pointed the book in her hand toward the coffee stand that was also for the customers of the Laundry Club. "Go grab us some, and we can discuss this Bobby Ray situation."

Before I'd come back to Kentucky, I didn't have a whole lot of true friends or confidants. Who'd have thought that I'd find a group of women that I'd come to trust and consider sisters in, of all places, a laundromat.

Abby and Queenie had already taken a seat near the washing machine I'd picked.

"You're doing his laundry?" Queenie held up a pair of the shorts I'd just bought.

"I'm not sure what Dottie said," I started, continuing before Queenie could interrupt, "but Joel over at Grassel's is in need of a mechanic. Bobby would be perfect for the job. I saw Joel over at the thrift shop, and he gave me his card to give to Bobby."

"She just said that some shady guy from your past showed up and she's sure he's only here to get money from you." Queenie crossed her arms and gave me a peeved look.

"To clear things up, you know that my family was killed in a house fire when I was a teenager." It was a memory that I didn't like to bring up, and the years after weren't as kind either. But it was my past, and I was good at putting that behind me until part of that past showed up this morning. "Bobby Ray was one of the foster kids in my last foster home. He had a full-time mechanic job and literally saved all his money. We'd spend hours talking about what we were going to do with our lives when we left Kentucky. He wanted to be a race car driver." I'd completely forgotten about that. I smiled at the passion he'd had for it. "Anyways, for my eighteenth birthday, he gave me a card with three thousand dollars in it. It was enough to get me a ticket on the Greyhound and make a down payment for flight attendant school."

"Dottie didn't make him sound that nice. She said his hair looked like cats had been sucking on it and his clothes…" She fanned her hand in front of her face.

"He's gotten older like me. His hair has thinned. And he walked here." I still couldn't believe it. "I let him take a shower while I grabbed some of Paul's old clothes out of the storage unit. Since I needed to get some laundry done, I figured I'd stop by the Tough Nickel and grab him a few pairs of shorts. That's all."

23

"You're so nice." Abby shrugged a shoulder to Queenie. "I bet he was thrilled to see you."

"He actually saw all the social media you'd been doing for the campground and read the article about Happy Trails in *National Parks of America* magazine. I don't mind him being here." I'd be eternally grateful for all the hard work that Abby did. "He said that he didn't come here to get paid back. He did mention he was down on his luck." I got some change out of my purse and slipped the coins into the machine's slot, selecting the hot cycle for whites. "But Joel Grassel said he was looking for a mechanic and would like to talk to Bobby Ray."

"Really?" She looked as pleased as a plump peach. "That's great. A long-lost family member!"

"Whoa!" I shook my head and ran my finger around the top of the mug. "We are far from family. He was really never around the foster family. Actually, we all tried to get jobs as soon as we could so we weren't around."

"You didn't like your foster family?" Abby questioned.

We all turned when we heard the bell over the door ding. It was Betts Hager, the owner of the Laundry Club and the wife of Pastor Lester.

"I liked them fine and would be forever grateful for them taking me in. But it's kind of hard when you're a teenager and strangers tell you how to act, and it really doesn't line up with the way your parents raised you." I scooted my chair closer to Queenie to make room for Betts.

"Where have you been lately?" Queenie was the one who kept tabs on everyone.

"I've been busier than a one-legged man in a kick-the-can contest." She huffed and melted back into the seat. "My cleaning side hustle has got me swamped. I really think people don't want to clean in this heat."

"I don't blame them. I'm having a hard time getting people to come to Jazzercise." Queenie took a drink of her coffee. "It'll break soon," she said, referring to the temperature.

"I've seen your flyers about the monthly campground get-together. Summer Sizzler party." She wiggled her brows. "Very creative."

"It's all Abby's marketing and Dottie's idea." I had to give credit where credit was due.

"Hey, I hear you've got a visitor," she said. "I called the campground office to talk to you, and Dottie told me all about him. I told her that sometimes people just want to reconnect."

"Spoken like a true preacher's wife," Queenie muttered.

Betts ignored her.

"What did you need?" I asked.

"I was wondering if you had any residents that wanted some part-time work. I need some help with cleaning. I've not been able to get my job at the church done, and Lester is working away on all the sermons since the tourists have been coming to church. That just tickles his fancy."

"What do you mean by 'part-time'?" I asked. It was no secret that I'd worked at the library for Abby to get a little extra cash. It helped pay back some of the millions of dollars Paul had taken from people. I'd made that my mission.

I knew I'd never make up what they lost on a financial, mental, or emotional level, but I had good intentions. Every time I could give something back, whether it was my time or money, it made my guilt about what he'd done a smidgen better.

"I need someone to clean a few apartments at the nursing home on the senior living side." She took her phone out of her purse. "I have two little old women who don't really require too much. They just love to talk so that really takes up time. Plus, I pick them up on Sunday to take them to church."

"Tilly and Olga?" I asked. I remembered them from church because not only were they the cutest of best friends, but they talked my head off once. I admit that, since then, I'd kept my head down and avoided them.

"That's them." She laughed. "Seriously, they barely have trash that needs to be emptied. But once a week, I'm there. Truthfully, I feel bad for taking their money because I feel like they are paying me just to talk to them."

"I can do it. It gets me out of the campground during this hot weather, and I can work in air-conditioning." It sounded like a pretty easy part-time job to me, and I liked visiting with the women at church.

"Are you sure?" Betts's voice took an upswing.

"Absolutely. I can help you clean until your other businesses slow down for you. When do I start?" I asked.

"This afternoon too early?" She gave me a pouty look.

"No. I can do it," I said and watched her face soften.

"Seriously, you have no idea how much time that frees up for me. This afternoon is Tammy Jo Bentley's house. Now I can stay here and do all the necessary work for the laundromat." She looked behind her. "Just like everything else, it's really booming in here."

"Tammy Jo?" Queenie's nose curled. "She was down at the Smelly Dog with that designer pooch of hers." Queenie's eyes rolled. "Fi-fi," she said with some sort of fancy, rich woman's accent.

"I heard about that." Betts snapped her fingers. Her face flushed when we all looked at her. "Just because I'm a preacher's wife doesn't mean I'm not privy to gossip."

"You go on and tell it then," Queenie encouraged her.

"I said I hear gossip, not take part in telling it." Betts recovered herself as we all laughed.

"What happened?" Abby scooted to the edge of her chair in anticipation before she took her phone out. "Hashtag Smelly Dog. Hashtag Normal. Get your dog groomed while hashtag hiking."

"You know Ethel Biddle don't like no one telling her how to cut her clients. Well, I heard Tammy Jo told Ethel how she wanted that poodle cut. When Ethel shaved the pom-pom off that dog's tail, Tammy Jo lost her ever-loving mind right there in the Smelly Dog."

"I know Tammy is par-ti-cu-lar about that dog." Betts lifted her chin up and down slowly. "She brought it to church."

Queenie and Abby gasped.

"Right into Sunday School. Missy King's eyes blew up like two balloons. When Lester told Tammy Jo that she couldn't bring the dog because of Missy King's allergies, she had the nerve to ask Missy King to leave the congregation," Betts said, dropping her jaw. "After she said that to Missy, I swear Missy said things that would make the devil himself blush."

Another round of collective gasps came from Queenie and Abby.

"You ain't allergic to dogs, are you?" Betts turned to me. "'Cause if you are, I suggest you take you a couple of antihistamines before you go. I've got a box in the glove compartment. I take a couple before I go in just for good measure."

"No." I shook my head. "I don't ever recall any allergies."

"Good. I'm so happy you can start today. In case you did say yes, I put together a list of what needs to be cleaned today. It's pretty simple. Are you sure you're okay?" she asked.

"I'm fine," I assured her.

"Mmmhhhh." She pulled a notebook out of her purse. "Here is a list of things she likes. And I check them off as I go because she's strange and will go over your work. Also, you can take my van, and I'll take your car. We can switch up sometime later." She dug deep in her purse and pulled out a set of keys. "I just take the pushcart out of the back, load it up, and push it all around the house."

It sounded easy enough, and the list didn't look so bad. I pulled my keys out of my pocket and traded with her.

"While I'm here, don't forget we have book club this week, but I thought we could go ahead and talk about next month's book while we are together." Abby looked at each of us individually, and when we all nodded, she continued, "Great. I thought, since it is the end of summer and it's so hot, we could pick *Heated Passion*."

"Geez Louise, Abby." Queenie's distaste for the book was written all over her face. "Did you get that recommendation from Jean's Beauty Shop? Because all I heard about down there while they were dyeing my roots was how much they couldn't put it down."

"Then it's a good book?" I questioned.

"If you like that sort." Queenie turned away and folded her arms across her chest—the only way she knew how to protest.

"If you have a better pick, let's hear it," Betts said, trying to keep the peace.

"Nope. You've done decided. I can't guarantee I can finish it in time. I'm pretty busy at Jazzercise." She blinked several times.

Betts looked down at her phone when it chirped. Abby took the time to post to social media.

"I thought you just said Jazzercise was slow?" Abby didn't look up from her phone. "Hashtag book club meeting at hashtag the Laundry Club."

"Oh, no." Betts stood up and put her phone back in her purse. "Lester just texted me. He's on his way to the hospital. Ron Randal has burnt his hand, and I've got to go look after his boys."

"Is he okay?" I asked.

"Lester didn't say. I've got to go. I'll text y'all about his condition when I hear." She darted through the Laundry Club and out the door.

My stomach did a flip-flop wondering if Ty Randal would come visit his dad from San Francisco. Not that I had a thing for Ty. There just seemed to be something unsaid between us when he left town.

CHAPTER FOUR

After I finished my laundry, I decided to walk down to Normal Diner, the diner Ron Randal owned. If I was going to clean someone else's toilet, I was going to need a shot of something good. Normal Diner was the perfect place for that. There was a big part of me that wanted to hear about Ron's accident too.

The diner was just as cute and southern as the other downtown shops. It was your standard greasy spoon with homecooked meals and was a diamond in the rough. The L-shaped diner had a row of stools against a counter to the left and a few booths along the right side in front of a wall of windows.

Every chair and booth had sparkly, fake leather vinyl that'd seen better days, but I chalked it up to adding character to the place. It was a hole-in-the-wall that was a treasure to find.

"Hey, Trudy," I called to the young waitress behind the counter when our eyes met. Her dishwater blonde hair was pulled back into a ponytail. An apron was tied around her full waist. There was a big smile on her face.

"Mae," she gasped. "Did you hear about Ron?" she asked, leaning her five-foot, eight-inch frame on the counter.

"I did. It's awful." I shook my head. "I was over at the Laundry Club, and Betts Hager got the call. How is he?" I eased down onto the last stool at the end of the counter.

Trudy lifted the lid on the glass pie stand in front of my seat and scooped out a piece of peach cobbler, setting the plate in front of me.

"He was frying some catfish, and he got to talking through the window to the regular old geezers who come in here. They were gabbing about hunting season, and Ron forgot about the fish. The fire alarms went off, and without thinking, he grabbed the fryer basket with his bare hands." She shook her head and put a napkin and fork in front of me. "I'd warned him so many times that he needed new ones with the grip handles that don't get hot, but he never listens to me. Nobody ever listens to me," she grumbled, wiping down the spot next to me after the customer left.

Trudy swiped his ticket and money, putting it in the front pocket of her apron.

"You enjoy that. Carol down at the farmers market sold Ron her fresh peaches, and it's to die for. Of course, if you talked to Pam Purcell, she'd say that her peaches are better. But they ain't." She grabbed a wet rag from behind the counter and wiped down the counter. "Plus, Pam's cost more. I don't know why. They grow in the same limestone and soil. Watered with the same tap water."

She rambled on about people I didn't even know. I nodded like I completely understood her and took a bite of the pie.

When she came up for air, I said, "I don't know Pam or her peaches, but Carol's are delicious. Did you call Ty?"

Trudy stopped dead in her tracks. She swung her hip to the right and planted a hand on her waist.

"Mae West." She shook a finger at me with her free hand. "You've got something for him, don't you?"

"Who do you have something for?" Detective Hank Sharp sat down on the empty stool next to me.

"Ty Randal." Trudy shimmied her shoulders.

"No, I don't. I just asked if someone had called Ty about his dad. That's all." I had no idea why I was explaining myself to Detective Hank, as I liked to call him. Although the last time Ty was in town, the uncomfortable situation I'd thought about earlier was interrupted by an unexpected visit from Detective Hank.

"What about Ron?" Hank asked. He'd obviously not been privy to the gossip about Ron's fryer incident.

"Didn't you hear?" Trudy scooped Hank a big piece of cobbler and put it in front of him. "He got real badly burned on his hand. Had to go to the emergency room." She nodded with wide eyes.

"Carol's peaches?" he asked between bites.

"Mmhhhmmmm," Trudy hummed and grabbed a pot of coffee. She walked down the long counter to refill all the mugs lined up, leaving me alone with Hank.

"You've got a thing for Ty Randal?" Hank turned his head, his green eyes piercing through me.

"Are you serious?" I blew him off. "His father is raising his two younger brothers. He's in the hospital. The last time Ron Randal was in the hospital..."

"The prodigal son arrived home to save the day. Or should I say diner?" he said, trying to joke.

"I hardly think Ron's open-heart surgery is something to be made fun of. Besides, Ty did come back here to run the diner and raise his brothers. Remember, their mother died years ago of cancer. You could have a little sympathy." I took the last bite of cobbler and pushed the plate away, taking a five-dollar bill from my pocket. I stood and dropped the money on the counter. "It was good seeing you, Detective Hank."

"Did you forget that Ron had a heart attack because your ex-husband almost took this diner from him?" Hank's jaw tensed.

"You know what?" I sucked in a deep breath, calming myself. "Never mind. I don't have time to fuss with you."

"What?" He smiled. His pearly white teeth, green eyes, and black hair against his olive skin were almost perfection, if only he didn't have this macho attitude. "I gave you a coffeemaker as a peace offering."

"What's your problem with Ty Randal?" I asked.

"I don't have a problem with Ty," he said, trying to convince me, but I'd seen them together when Ty was in town, and there was definitely something off between them. His phone buzzed. He yanked it out of the clip on his belt and took a long look at it before he put it back.

"I don't believe you." I shrugged.

"Don't be going around using those investigation skills you think you've got, trying to dig up something that's not there," he warned, reminding me how I'd stuck my nose into the death of my ex-husband. "Gotta go. Duty calls."

"What? A bear breaking into someone's car?" I joked and watched him get up.

"Not on park duty today." He wasn't going to give me any juicy gossip about the text. "Thanks, Trudy. Loved the cobbler."

I twisted the stool around and watched Hank leave the diner. From the first day we met, there'd been a little tension. There was tension between us when we were alone, not talking about his job, and there was tension when we were alone, talking about his job. It was something I'd yet to put my finger on but didn't go unnoticed.

To let my cobbler digest before I headed over to Tammy Jo's to clean her toilets, I decided to go to the hospital to see Ron Randal's condition for myself. I'd actually gotten close to Ron since I moved to Normal. Maybe it was his sad story and how I admired him for raising his sons on his own while running a business. Not that his oldest son, Ty, with his messy blond hair, crystal-blue eyes, and Southern charm, had anything to do with my feelings.

I gulped back the images of the last time I'd seen Ty. We were interrupted by my lawyer, Stanley. Stanley had popped into Happy Trails to tell me that he'd found a buyer for the campground.

At that time, everyone in Normal and Happy Trails thought I was staying. Stanley didn't know that I'd already decided to stay, but that's not what Ty heard. He must've thought I was abandoning the campground like my deceased ex-husband had done, making me no different from Paul. But he didn't stick around to hear me tell Stanley that I wasn't selling. I'd found a home and friends in Normal, something that didn't have a price.

When I went to tell Ty, he was nowhere to be found. The next day I found out that, since his dad was home and better, he'd gone back to San Francisco, where he had been a pretty popular chef. When I saw Ron in the diner and a few times at Happy Trails when he'd brought Ty's two younger brothers fishing, I couldn't bring myself to ask about Ty. Surely, Ty knew from his dad that I didn't sell the campground, and that was now water under the bridge.

Lester Hager was in the emergency waiting room. He stood up to greet me. I motioned for him to sit back down. He looked tired. The dark circles under his eyes were a shade of gray. He had black hair that was always so neatly parted to the right and clean-cut. He stood about six foot and had a slight gut that I was sure came from all the good food the Bible Thumpers, what we called the church ladies, made. He and Betts were young, and they had so many great ideas for the community and the world.

"Pastor," I greeted him, sitting on the edge of the chair next to his. "How's Ron?"

"They are working on getting the skin cleaned up so they can bandage it. They are talking skin grafts and some sort of oxygen chamber. Those poor kids." He folded his hands in his lap. "I've got Betts staying over at his house. I know she's got all sorts of houses to clean and she's just a saint."

"She is. We are glad to have you both here in Normal." I sat back. I wasn't sure how long I was going to stay, but he seemed like he could use the company. "Can I get you something?"

"Nah. I'm good." His phone rang. "It's Ty." He stood up and walked across the emergency room where there was a little more privacy.

The mention of his name made my stomach drop. I sucked in a deep breath to get oxygen to my brain. While he talked, people started to show up: Alvin Deters, owner of Deters's Feed-N-Seed; Buck, owner of the Tough Nickel; and Joel Grassel, owner of Grassel's Gas Station. They were regulars at the diner as well as lifelong friends of Ron.

"Any news?" Alvin asked. The other two looked at me over his shoulder.

"I just got here. Pastor said that they are trying to clean it up, but nothing yet." I gestured where Pastor had walked away. "Ty was calling, so he stepped away."

"The boys?" Joel asked.

"Betts is with them." It was times like these where all the gossip and tales weren't important. This was when the community came together. I should know. Even after what Paul had done to them, they still accepted me and supported everything I needed to bring the campground back to life.

"I'm going to head down to the cafeteria and get a cup of coffee. Anyone want anything?" Buck asked his friends.

"I'll go with you. They got good coffee." Joel nodded. All three of them went to get coffee, and Pastor was still on the phone.

"Family of Ron Randal," a nurse called from the sliding-glass window.

"I'm with Ron." I wasn't family, but there was no family and Pastor didn't look over.

"He can have a visitor now." She pushed a button and the double doors slowly started to open. She met me on the other side. "He's going to need a minor surgery. I just wanted to warn you before you see him. He's in a lot of pain."

I followed her down the hall. She stopped in front of room ten, whipping the curtain open.

"Mae?" He had a surprised look on his face. His hand was dangling up in the air like it was on a hook. When he tried to push himself up a little, a groan escaped him. "I wasn't sure who was out there. They said someone was here."

"You just lie there and don't move," I instructed him. "You've got a whole crew out there." I walked over to his bed. "Everyone went to get coffee, so you got me." I smiled. "How are you?"

"From what I hear, I've got to have a quick surgery. Then they want to put me back in that darn nursing home for physical therapy." He seemed to be in better spirits than I expected. "I guess I'm going to have to find a babysitter for the boys."

"I'm not much of a babysitter, but they can stay with me until we can find someone. I know that Betts has them now, and really, she's the best." Not that I had to convince him, but I was putting my foot in my mouth as soon as I opened it. I didn't know a thing about kids.

"She's so busy. I mean, the boys know the campground, and you really don't have to watch them much. I can get Betts to clean Ty's camper." He let out a long sigh. "Ty. Has anyone called him?"

"Pastor was on the phone with him when the nurse called for someone to come back." Just as the words left my mouth, Lester came into the room.

"Pastor Lester, thank you for coming." Ron was still a polite man under these circumstances. "Mae said you talked to Ty."

"Yes. He's booked a plane ticket for tomorrow. He's getting in around ten in the morning. Flying into the Bluegrass Airport."

I tried to keep my face from doing some sort of contortion while I listened to Lester give the details of Ty's arrival.

"I'd be happy to pick him up from the airport, but Betts and I have a funeral at church. Your younger boys can go to the children's room and play. Me and Betts love having them."

"Mae, can you get him?" Ron asked.

"Me?" My eyes jumped open. "Yeah, sure. I can take the boys with me."

"They wouldn't do good on the couple hours' drive. They can stay back at the campground with Henry." Ron was much more trusting of Henry than I would be, but then again, they were his kids. "I hate to ask you to do that, keep the boys tonight, and clean Ty's camper. That's a lot."

"I live there anyways." I gulped. What had I just done to myself? "It's not a problem."

When the other men came in, I excused myself, but not before Pastor Lester gave me the information I needed to pick up Ty. The entire way across Normal to Tammy Jo Bentley's house, I rehearsed how I was going to greet Ty when I did pick him up. I found myself apologizing to my imaginary passenger.

CHAPTER FIVE

G etting used to driving Betts's minivan was my first adventure of the afternoon, but that was only the beginning. I pulled into Tammy Jo's neighborhood and noticed all the beautifully manicured green lawns with billowing white dogwoods.

Tammy Jo Bentley's house was on the right behind a big concrete wall with a wrought iron gate with a B in the middle. The gates started to open before I could even push the button to announce my arrival. Betts didn't tell me that Tammy Jo obviously had money.

Right off the bat, I recognized the black car parked close to the house. It was Hank Sharp's. Was the text he'd gotten at the diner about Tammy Jo? There was only one way to find out.

I opened the back of the van and looked down Betts's list.

"'Vacuum the vents.'" I looked into the back and took out the cart, popping it into the locked position. I dragged out the vacuum and stuck it on the bottom of the cart. "'Dust all furniture and the baseboards in the family room. Be sure to clean the kitchen and the dining room thoroughly along with the guest bathroom on the first floor. No other rooms this week,'" I read out loud.

There were a couple of buckets that had tags with names attached to the handles. There was one for TJB, which I figured had to be Tammy

Jo's. When I looked into it, there appeared to be everything I needed—from furniture polish to toilet cleaner.

"Betts, how are you doing?" Hank Sharp's voice startled me. I jumped around. Both of us were equally shocked to be standing in front of the other. "Mae?"

Behind him stood a woman about five feet, ten inches tall with frosted blond hair that was short on the side but styled high on top. Back in my day, we'd called that the public-school poof. She wore a pair of pleated white pants along with a sleeveless, hot-pink polka dot shirt. The poodle she was holding had on a bow the same color pink as Tammy Jo's polka dots.

Fifi.

"Who are you?" Tammy Jo eyed me suspiciously and pulled her dog closer to her like I was some dog thief.

The dog yipped and wiggled around in Tammy Jo's arms before it squirmed right on out, scurrying over to me. A man walked out the front door and stood on the porch.

"Fifi!" Tammy Jo screamed and bolted down the steps, almost walking out of her heeled shoes with the pink pom-poms on the top. "What did mama teach you about stranger danger?"

Apparently, Fifi was fond of me. She continued to jump nearly up to my waist, her furless tail helicoptering around each time. I bent down to give a quick little rub down her back before Tammy Jo jerked her back up into her arms. The man stood close to her side. He rubbed Fifi like my smell had harmed her and he was checking to see if she was okay.

"This is Mae West, owner of Happy Trails, and I'd like to know what she's doing here too." Hank glared at me suspiciously. "Mae, this is Norman Pettleman. He's an insurance man in town."

Norman offered a slight smile. His neat and tidy short blond hair was parted to the side with such precise detail that the part showed his scalp. He could use a little sun, I thought, looking at his pale skin. The light-brown suit seemed to hang off of him. I'd heard of Norman Pettleman. He'd actually left a message on the Happy Trails answering machine about insurance for the campground, but I went to Heidelman Insurance Agency. I felt like Mr. Heidelman gave me a good deal since I ended up giving him a good deal on the new yearly lease for his lot space.

"Nice to meet you." I nodded at Norman. He lifted his dark-brown briefcase toward me in a welcoming way. "I'm filling in for Betts Hager while she takes care of Ron Randal's boys." I pushed the toe of my shoe down on the brake of the cart to release it and began to push it around to the side of the house where Betts had written to enter.

"Wait just a second." Tammy Jo's voice was terse. Her hand lifted and tried like heck to push back some of her bangs, but the hairspray was like cement. I wondered if the sun was going to bake her hair in that position.

"She didn't tell me anything about this. I don't know your cleaning skills. I have a huge party here tomorrow with the local KKA, and I can't let anything go wrong." Tammy Jo wore a bird-thin scowl on her heavily rouged lips. Her lashes fluttered as fast as a hummingbird's wings.

"KKA?" I asked. It didn't matter, but my curiosity got to me.

"Kentucky Kennel A-soc-ee-ation." She announced her words just like a true southerner, drawing out each syllable. "I've spent the better part of the last year convincing them to let me host the annual meeting, and I've got to have an immaculate house." Her eyes drew up and down me, as if she were assessing my cleanliness. "And an immaculate Fifi." She put the poodle up to her face, making kissy noises.

"I promise you that I'll do a wonderful job." Not that I wanted to kiss Miss Fancy-Pants's hiney in front of Hank Sharp. By the look on his face, he was clearly enjoying this. "I assured Betts I'd take care of you."

Norman spoke up. "It's fine. Let her do her job. We don't have time between now and tomorrow to find someone you think can clean better."

"Hank?" She looked at him like his opinion was the only one that mattered and he was going to give me a recommendation right on the spot.

"Aww, she checks out fine, Mrs. Bentley." His Southern drawl was as thick and sweet as molasses.

"Fine. But you need to get up that dirt stain on my carpet in front of the mantle. Do you got it?" She glared at me. I nodded. "Go on then. And stay out of my way," she threatened before I got the cart pushed around the corner of the house.

There were big white tents set up in the backyard. In front of each tent was a big ice block with ice carvers chipping away at them. The middle tent ice sculpture was definitely in the image of Fifi. The Daniel Boone National Forest was the backdrop beyond the tents, and it was breathtaking.

I stopped pushing the cart when I noticed there were three doors. I looked around the cart for Betts's notebook to see exactly which door I was supposed to use. Heavens to Betsy, I go through the wrong door. Tammy Jo might have Hank arrest me for trespassing.

I locked the cart's wheels and hurried back to the van, almost running smack-dab into a lanky gal with long brown hair wearing light-pink scrubs and a slightly taller man in a blue jumpsuit.

"I'm sorry." I tucked my head in apology when I saw them jump apart, making me think I'd clearly interrupted something private.

The notebook was right inside the backdoor of the van. I grabbed it and headed back around the house, a little more cautious this time. Luckily, the guy and gal were gone. The man in the blue jumpsuit was hunkered over the flower garden next to the deck, and the young woman was nowhere in sight.

In the instructions, Betts said to use the middle door. Once inside, the wheels on the metal cart squeaked across the marble floor with each rotation. I kept looking back to make sure the wheels didn't leave some sort of mark. That'd make extra work, and I was counting the hours until I got out of there.

The kitchen didn't take too long to clean. It didn't look like there'd been much cooking going on in there. I made quick work of the bathroom too.

The family room had tall ceilings with a big chandelier hanging in the middle. There were three white leather couches with a coffee table in front of each one. There were crystal and china poodle knickknacks nestled all over the room. My insides groaned at the thought of wiping all of them down by hand.

Betts had written to dust all the furniture and baseboards before vacuuming. There was a furniture polish with a hand mitt stuck on top. I pushed my hand into the mitt and sprayed polish on the glove. It was Tammy Jo's preferred method for dusting. I rolled my eyes and went over all the little figurines, followed by the larger pieces of furniture. Betts was right. There was a lot of dust.

"You do know that Tammy likes the furniture dusted before you vacuum." The same woman I'd seen outside with the long brown hair and pink scrubs walked through the double doors to the deck just outside of the family room. She ran a finger down the coffee table and held it up into the air to get a look. "Not bad. Don't forget the watch on the mantle."

She and I both looked over at the marble mantle. The only object displayed was a glass dome with what looked like a pocket watch inside.

"I won't. Tammy Jo asked me to get the dirt stain in front of it." I walked over to look at the stain. Nothing that a little water couldn't get up.

The young woman followed me. There was a strange look on her face when she noticed the stain.

"It's just dirt, I think." I bent down to make sure it wasn't something of Fifi's, like poop. Upon closer inspection, it was just dried mud.

She picked up her foot and looked at the bottom of her shoe, repeating the process with the other.

"I'm not sure how that got there." Her brows furrowed with a worried look.

"What's so special about that?" I asked, taking the conversation back to the watch. There wasn't anything special about the dirty carpet. I wasn't sure why she was so concerned.

"It's a treasured family heirloom Tammy Jo acquired from Harrison Bentley." She walked closer to it and gazed at it. I assumed she was talking about Tammy Jo's husband. And from the way it sounded, I assumed Harrison was dead. "It's worth 2.2 million dollars."

I was so shocked that you could've knocked me over with a feather.

"You're joking." I lifted a brow and took a little more interest in it. I walked over. "It doesn't look special."

It was a standard round gold pocket watch with a white background and four circles on its face. One of the circles had numbers; the one next to it had Roman numerals; and the other two had little black lines. There were black numbers around the entire circumference of the face. The gold chain had what looked like a small blue wand at the end. Nothing special to me.

"I'd never joke about 2.2 million dollars. Tammy Jo has a person who comes every morning, puts on a pair of white gloves, lifts the lid, and uses the watch-winding key to wind it." She inhaled deeply. "It's special because the different ticks help train Fifi. Since Tammy Jo doesn't have children, she left it to Fifi and any offspring she might have."

"Who might have children?" I rubbed my temples, trying to wrap my head around the concept of a 2.2-million-dollar watch that should clearly be in some sort of museum.

"Fifi." The woman said this as if it was no big deal that a dog was the beneficiary of this watch. "My job is to keep Fifi in perfect health." She drew her hands in front of her, clasping them at her waist. "We are going to be meeting people who might have a potential sire for our dear Fifi."

"What exactly is your job title?" My right eyebrow rose.

She perked up a little. "I'm Fifi's nanny."

"You're joking, right?" My eyes creased with amusement.

"I'd never joke about Fifi." Her jaw tensed.

"Nanny for a dog?" I questioned. How much did that gig pay?

"Yes. Fifi is very special. She comes from a long line of distinguished breeding. She has to have the perfect amount of play, food, and sleep time." She spoke with pride. This girl was serious. "I'm thrilled to have been here since the beginning. She'll be four this fall. We are hoping to breed her soon since she's the perfect age."

"What makes this watch worth so much money?" I asked.

As hard as I tried, I couldn't take my eyes off it. Nor could I even fathom what state of mind Tammy Jo had been in when leaving it to a dog. Not that I didn't love dogs. I did; I just did not want one for myself.

"It's got very detailed and complicated George Daniel parts. He was a famous watchmaker. There aren't many around, and they have so many details that are fascinating." She was practically salivating at the mouth. "All of his watches are done by hand. Truly works of art. Now that Tammy Jo has mortgaged the entire estate to see to it that Fifi's DNA can be cloned to continue the breeding line, she's very particular about the watch."

While she told me the history of the watch, I couldn't help but notice Hank, Tammy Jo, minus Fifi, and Norman, outside on the lawn. Tammy Jo was pointing to different things as Hank nodded.

"Clone the dog?" I laughed. Tammy Jo Bentley was a whack job. By the look on the woman's face, she didn't find it at all funny. "According to the 2.2-million-dollar watch, I've got to finish cleaning this house. Don't you have to get back to Fifi?" I asked when I heard a door shut down the hall, followed by a woman's voice.

"She's napping." The dog nanny's face didn't move, but her eyes shifted toward the woman talking. "She gets a midmorning nap and a late afternoon nap." She inhaled deeply and glanced over at the window. I looked to see what—or who—she was watching.

I didn't see Hank, Tammy Jo, or Norman, but I did see the man in the blue jumpsuit that I'd seen her talking to earlier.

When he walked out of view, she looked back at me. "Where's Betts?"

"She had to take care of some church people." It was a short and simple answer. I didn't have time for chitchat. I put the polish back in the cart and got the vacuum.

"The kitchen looks good," she said as if she'd inspected my work. "Please tell Betts we miss her."

"What's your name?" I asked. I wanted to make sure I got it right so, when I went back to the Laundry Club and told this ridiculous story, I'd get it right. The women wouldn't believe this one. Maybe Betts would since she's cleaned here, but she'd never tell them. That's why it was my duty to get it all straight.

"Camille Braun." She turned and saw the man in the window again. This time he saw her, and they locked eyes. "Goodbye," she whispered and drifted out the double doors to the back deck where she'd come in from.

The outlet for the vacuum cleaner was next to the window. I looked out and saw the man in the blue jumpsuit walking down the back of the house and then slipping into one of the doors. I continued to watch Camille. She took the steps to the right of the deck. At the bottom, she looked around before she went through the same door as the man.

"Interesting," I said, plugging in the vacuum. I wondered if the gardener and the nanny were having a secret rendezvous, which would add some juicy gossip to my tale for the girls.

I went back to the bucket on the cart and took out the screwdriver so I could unscrew the wall vents since Betts had specifically said to get those vacuumed. I went back to where the sweeper was plugged in and got down on my knees to unscrew the first vent.

At first, I thought the voices I'd heard were coming from a television. I pulled back, resting on my haunches, and listened. I bent toward the vent and could clearly hear a conversation. I wondered if it was the dog nanny and the gardener.

"My darling Camille," the voice coming through the vent said. "I forgive you. Please, let's put it behind us."

"I can't do that, Ralphie. We'll never be an item. I have so much expected of me and the status of my position here. Tammy Jo will never accept us. If she finds out, she'll fire both of us. I can't let that happen. I love Fifi and her future is my future's security." Camille was a tough cookie, I thought. "You were a fling. You need to know that."

"You are evil. You will regret your treatment of me. One day, you'll get what's coming to you because you are a greedy tramp. Get out of my face," he spat back at her. I bent down a little closer to see if I could hear the murmur that sounded like someone crying.

There were sounds of scrambling, and I quickly turned the vacuum on to clean around the inside of the vent. The door to the deck flew open. Camille rushed through the family room with her hands covering her face.

CHAPTER SIX

"You mean to tell me that you took the time to go to the diner and didn't find out a single thing about Ron Randal?" Dottie asked when I got back to the office at Happy Trails Campground. "Queenie said you were in there awhile."

"Are you going to let me finish telling you before you interrupt me?" I asked. Dottie was very good at trying to jump ahead in the story someone was telling her. "I was actually eating a piece of peach cobbler." I thumbed through the reservations to see what available campers we had for Bobby Ray. I left out the part about seeing Hank because Dottie would've been all over that.

"Carol's or Pam's peaches?" she asked.

"Carol's." I laughed. Living in Kentucky as an adult was really teaching me just how small the towns were in the state. With that came all the gossip and being in everyone's business.

"Pam is going to have a conniption. I can see it now. Both of them swingin' their bibles at their Bible Thumpers meeting." Dottie shook her head, referring to Betts Hager's bible club that supplied all the food for local events, ministered to criminals at the jails, and other various things. Dottie handed me a set of keys. "I know you're looking through the reservations to find your thieving friend a camper. Let him have this one."

"You do have a soft spot." I took the keys. "He's not a thief. Be nice. I gave him the money back like you suggested. That should make you feel better."

"It don't. Did you see how comfortable he was out there?" She meandered over to the window, and I followed her.

"Those khakis," I groaned when I noticed Bobby Ray had taken a pair of scissors to them, making them the shortest khaki shorts I'd ever seen. "They were expensive."

What was I expecting? Paul and Bobby Ray were from two different planets. I should've realized that, once I'd given them to Bobby Ray, they'd be regarded as a gift, not a loan. I shrugged it off. What was I going to do with them anyways?

"Back to Ron." I had to forget Bobby for a minute. "I've also got to clean Ty's camper. Betts is going to keep the boys for Ron tonight." My face flushed. "I'm picking up Ty at the airport in the morning."

"May-bell-ine." She tried to use her best Bobby Ray voice. "You're gonna have to juggle two men that are swooned over you. Hank Sharp and Ty Randal. They are hankerin'."

"I'm certain Hank Sharp isn't hankerin'," I said sarcastically. "I saw him today at Tammy Jo Bentley's house."

"My word." Dottie jerked back and looked at me. "What on earth were you doing at that woman's house? Don't you know she's a couple buckets of crazy?"

"Betts had gotten the phone call about the Randal boys, and she was supposed to go to Tammy's to clean since Tammy is hosting the Kentucky Kennel Association tomorrow."

She snarled. "You know, she can be real nasty about that dog of hers."

"Fifi." I laughed a belly laugh. "I swear. That dog is treated better than a human child. It sure was something to see."

"Did you see the dog?" she asked.

"I did. I think it actually liked me." It was a cute little dog.

TONYA KAPPES

"Is the puff ball at the tip of her tail really shaved?" There was a disturbing giddiness in her tone.

"Yes." I grinned. "I'd heard about what happened at Smelly Dog, and I couldn't stop looking at it. I mean, Fifi has this big puffball here, here, and here, not to mention several on her legs." I pointed to all the places.

We had a good laugh.

"Seriously though, did you know that Tammy Jo has a 2.2-million-dollar pocket watch on her mantle?" I still couldn't believe it.

"Hmmm." Lines creased in her forehead. Apparently, she didn't have anything to say about that.

"She's left it to Fifi and any puppies she has." I couldn't explain enough how crazy this sounded to me. "Not to charity or even family."

"Mae, she's tighter than a wet bathing suit on a long ride home." Her red curls bounced as she talked. "She's got family members that she fell out with a long time ago. A daughter."

My eyes widened.

"Where is the daughter?" I asked.

"Beats me." She shrugged, a delicate movement that spoke volumes.

I had a niggling suspicion that she knew more than she was telling. She'd gone back to leaning over the computer on her desk. It was weird that she wasn't gossiping about it. I decided to change the subject.

"How are the plans for the Summer Sizzler?" I asked and walked into the storage closet. There were camper sets we let campers rent or purchase. The sets were different depending on what they needed. We had toothbrushes, sheets, towels, bathing suits. I grabbed the deluxe for Bobby Ray. It included shampoos, razors, and all the fixin's.

"Comin' along good. I've got to do some setup over the next couple of days, but it's all ready to go. I put the decorations in one of the storage units so they are out of the way. We had four campers pull in today. I told them about how we do supper around here and invited them to participate. I think I saw two of the families head on out to Daniel Boone National Forest."

We made plans to hang out tonight at supper before I headed on

48

over to the lake to get Bobby Ray and take him to his housing for the next couple of days.

There were a couple of different buildings on the property besides the office and a few covered picnic shelters. We had a recreation room for games and family fun. There was an assortment of video games, a Ping-Pong table, hula hoops, basketballs, dodgeballs, kickballs, jump ropes, and a snack station. There was a laundry room with washers and dryers. Instead of a pool, we had a fishing lake with a fountain aeration system surrounded by a nice sandy beach. On days I was just lollygagging around, I was in a chair with my eyes closed to the sun. It was a little too hot to do that these last few weeks of summer.

The campers must've felt the same way because the lake was full of swimmers and people circling the lake in pedal boats. I'd been expecting to see my insurance man here any day. He and his wife rented a lot here year-round. I'd asked him to get an insurance proposal together for me about putting in a pool, but I was sure the liability would be through the roof.

"Catch anything?" I asked when I walked up to Henry and Bobby Ray.

"Nah. We just shootin' the breeze," Henry said. Bobby Ray was right up his alley. Both men were simple and seemed to enjoy the slow life.

"I've got you a bungalow." I dangled the key in the air. "And a job." I took Joel's business card out and handed it to him.

"Which bungalow? And what job?" Henry asked as if I were giving his job to Bobby Ray.

"Number Three." I knew Henry loved that one. "And Grassel's Gas Station as a mechanic."

"My favorite bungalow." Henry smacked Bobby Ray on the back. "It's perfect for one. It's got the best sunrise and sunset. The view of the park is breathtaking. And Joel Grassel will be a good man to work for."

"I'm looking forward to it. Both of them." Bobby Ray jerked the line of his rod and rapidly rolled in the reel. "I'm looking forward to eating this guy." He pulled in a largemouth bass that was going to taste great on the open campfire.

Bobby Ray was pretty pleased with the bungalow setup. It was round with a kitchen and bathroom in the middle. It had a perfect view from every window. While I let him get settled in, I jumped into the golf cart to head back to the office to grab a bucket of supplies to clean Ty's camper.

We sold cleaning supplies for the campers to make cleaning easier for them. After I got what I needed, I grabbed Ty's extra set of keys with the T key ring. I couldn't help but smile and wonder what his life looked like as the head chef of some fancy San Francisco restaurant.

"You need help with Ty's camper?" Dottie asked as a plume of smoke rolled out of her mouth. She was sitting outside under her awning, enjoying her cigarette. Her twinkle lights were already on, and she was ready for suppertime.

I'd told her a million times she needed to quit. She said it's her one pleasure in life. Who was I to take that away from her? It was only out of love for her that I wanted her to be healthy.

"I think I got it." I held up the cleaning supplies. I realized I wanted to do it myself for some weird reason. She muttered something under her breath that I was sure I didn't want to hear. She was always rambling on about how I needed to find a man when she'd obviously forgotten what the last one had done over the past five years of my life.

Ty's camper was a pull behind. It was yellow with a red stripe. He paid a lot fee to keep it there. A few weeks after he'd gone back home, I'd gotten a wire transfer for a full year of lot fees. I never anticipated him coming back but figured his dad and brothers would use it to camp on the weekends. When they were here, it was nice to have the company. For some reason, I had hit it off with his family. I felt bad that Ty's mom had died and left Ron with two little boys. They'd had Ty's younger brothers later in life. One was in high school, and the other was in grade school.

My phone chirped a text alert. It was from Betts Hager. She said that she was happy to report that Tammy Jo was pleased with the cleaning and with how much Fifi liked me. She said to hold on to the check and she'd get it tomorrow.

I texted her back that I didn't get a check and would go back in the morning to get it on my way to the airport to pick up Ty.

As I was unlocking Ty's door, she texted back, "TY!!!!!", followed by a heart emoji.

I ignored her and the rest of the gals from the Laundry Club who texted me right after her. I wasn't sure why they were acting like there was something between me and Ty. In fact, when I first met him, he owed the campground three months of lot fees. It wasn't a pleasant exchange, and we certainly weren't an item. He didn't even say goodbye when he left.

I opened the door of Ty's camper, and the masculine smell nearly made me dizzy. My stomach tickled, and I found myself really excited for his arrival. I gulped back my feelings and got to work. Maybe the Laundry Club gals did see something I was desperately trying to hide.

The inside of his camper was just one room. There was a bed loft on the right that was over the hookup to pull the camper. There was a small built-in couch with an efficiency kitchen across from it. There was also a bathroom along the back. That was pretty much it besides a little storage. Perfect for a single man like Ty.

I found clean sheets and towels in the storage under the couch. After making the bed and doing a light dusting, there wasn't much left to do. Out of curiosity, I started to look through the drawers. There wasn't much in there, just some bottle openers, tools, lighters, and extension cords. There was a red-and-white-striped chair folded up in the corner, and I vividly remembered him sitting in it at night during the spring breeze. Not that I was always looking toward his camper. Not always. Just sometimes.

The last drawer I opened had a yearbook in it. I sat on the couch and flipped through the book. I giggled out loud when I saw Ty and his short hair. I couldn't even think of him without all that shaggy hair he had now. I read through a few of the notes and signatures. There was one that caught my eye. It had a bright-red lip stamp next to it.

"Nicki," I said and ran my finger across her lipstick print. "'We will always be *Ty'd* together.' Aren't you clever," I noted and continued to read the rest of her note, "'I can't wait to see where our future leads us in college. I love you.'" I about gagged when I noticed the three exclamation marks after the "I love you". I even rolled my eyes a couple of times.

I flipped back to the senior photos and dragged my finger along the names on every page until I came to the only Nicki in the senior class.

"Nicki Swaggert?" I asked in a hushed whisper, wondering if she was related to Dottie. She had to be.

I started comparing myself to this young girl, who probably didn't even look like this now. I mean, I didn't look like I did when I was a senior in high school. Still, she had a long thin neck and long blond hair parted to the side. Her smile melted into her blue eyes. Ty had blue eyes.

After staring at her for a few minutes and burning her face into my memory, I flipped through the clubs and the candid shots. I had to stop counting how many times I'd seen Nicki smiling next to everyone. Then... the Senior Superlatives.

Best Looking Couple went to Nicki Swaggert and Hank Sharp.

"Hank Sharp?" I gasped. "This is how Ty and Hank know each other."

I wondered if this Nicki was the source of the tension between them. When I heard some rumblings outside of the camper, I looked up. It was beginning to get dark. I'd let time fly by while I looked at the yearbook and made up things in my head.

I threw the book back in the drawer and took one last look around as I gathered up the supplies.

"There you are." Bobby Ray was walking around the corner of the camper when I locked Ty's door behind me. "Who lives there?" he asked.

"A camper who doesn't live here but rents full-time. He's coming in tomorrow and needed his camper cleaned." There was no sense in telling him about Ty. I was banking on Bobby Ray not being here long, and he didn't need to know any more about me. "Did you need something?"

"Yeah. Did you know that I've got to cook something for this campground dinner?" he asked a little frantically.

"Yes. But don't worry. I have some hot dogs you can contribute for us." I motioned for him to get in the golf cart.

I'd forgotten to explain that every night the campers are encouraged to participate in a progressive supper. Every camper cooks a different food at their campfire. They can take their plate around and sample everyone's dish. Some people do desserts while others do meats and the sides. It was a big hit and a fun way to get to know each other.

"How was the rest of your day?" I asked, making small talk.

"You've got a good thing goin' on here." Bobby nodded. "I really like that Henry. I hope you don't mind me just showing up."

"Not at all." I sucked in a deep breath, nearly choking on the late-day heat, and hoped it didn't show that I didn't want him to stay too long.

"I gave Joel Grassel a call. We are going to have a meetin' in a couple of days. Do you think you could take me?" he asked.

"I'd love to. Just be sure to let me know when." I parked the golf cart in front of my camper, and we headed inside. I opened the refrigerator to get the hot dogs.

"Are those crescent rolls?" he asked.

"Yes." I took out the can. "You want them?"

"Yes! I make the best campfire pigs in a blanket. That's perfect." He took the two cans I had and the two packs of hot dogs. "You coming?" He stopped shy of the door.

"I'm going to clean up a little. I cleaned a house and a camper today. I smell bad." I lifted up my arm and pretended to smell my armpit. "I'll see you in a few."

A few apparently meant the next day because, after I took a long hot shower, I lay down on the bed for a quick little rest and didn't wake up until the sun was peeking through the open blinds the next morning.

CHAPTER SEVEN

"Oh, no! No! No!" I jumped up when I realized that I'd fallen asleep before I'd set the alarm on my phone to go get Ty. According to the bright sun filtering into the camper, it was the next morning.

The Bluegrass Airport was two hours away, which meant I should've left about thirty minutes ago to make it there on time, and I'd yet to trade Betts for my car. It looked like I was going to have to drive the minivan to pick up Ty.

I took a quick shower and had to forget about doing my hair and makeup. It wasn't how I pictured myself when Ty saw me for the first time on this visit. A little lip gloss and some wet hair that'd turn to frizz in this heat was going to have to do.

Dottie waved her hand, a big cig stuck in between her fingers, when I passed her camper. I wanted so bad to stop and ask about Nicki, but there was no time for gossip.

Ty was standing by the curb outside the sliding doors at the arrival gate when I pulled up. I honked and waved only to be greeted by what I'd call shock and awe on his face. Those blue eyes popped against his tanned skin. The shaggy blond hair curled and framed his face. It was a little longer than he'd worn it in the spring, but it still looked tidy and handsome.

I threw the van into Park and jumped out.

"Welcome home." I clasped my hands in front of me to keep them from finding a mind of their own and flinging them around his neck. But my mind had another plan. As if in slow motion, I watched as my arms floated up in the air with each step my feet were taking to him, wrapping them around his neck.

"Mae, I'm a little shocked to see you here to pick me up." He used both hands to pat my back. I might've nuzzled him a little when I audibly inhaled to take in his smell—the same smell that permeated the inside of his camper. He took a step back.

"I'm sorry I'm late." I tucked a stray strand of my curly mess behind my ear. "I've been helping Betts clean, and I lost track of time this morning," I lied. I didn't want him to think I'd overslept and was scatterbrained. "Which reminds me, do you mind if we stop by Tammy Jo Bentley's to pick up a check on our way into Normal?"

"Not at all." He grabbed the big suitcase next to his feet. "I'm glad you brought Betts's van because all of these are mine." He turned and looked at the luggage behind him.

"Wow. I didn't realize your dad was that bad." I'd felt bad for not calling to check on Ron this morning on my way here. He must've gotten worse if Ty'd brought all this home for a visit.

"He's not. They moved him to the rehab center this morning. He's only going to be there a couple of days so they can keep an eye on the burn and skin graft and make sure it doesn't get infected." He picked up his luggage and put them in the back of the van, pushing the cleaning supplies closer to the front. "They are starting him on physical therapy to move his fingers and wrists, but they are things he can do at home once he learns them."

"That's great news." I tried not to seem so eager, but I felt like a schoolgirl. Kinda like Nicki. Inwardly, I groaned. Nicki. Ugh. "Are you staying a while or just bringing some things back?"

"Actually, I'm moving back." He didn't seem to be as upbeat as my heart.

"Really?" My voice was a little shaky. "Why? I thought you loved living there."

We got into the van. There was a slew of emotions rumbling up inside of me. Ones that I didn't recognize, and they almost scared me. Yes, he was super attractive, and if you asked any woman in Normal, they'd agree. But there was something about him actually living in Normal that kind of had me worried. I think in the back of my head I knew I could look at him and fantasize since I knew he was always going back to San Francisco. This time he wasn't going back.

"I do, but after I was here last spring helping dad raise the boys, I realized I'd missed out a lot on them growing up. They need as many adults in their lives as they can get, and I felt like I was ripping the family apart all over again. Sean is almost an adult, but Timmy needs me." He put his elbow on the windowsill, covering his mouth with his hand and staring out the window. "Enough about that. I'm here and staying. Just like you, Mae West."

"I wondered if you were going to bring that up." I gripped the wheel and steered the van onto the interstate that would take us back to the Daniel Boone National Forest. "I was going to explain what you'd overheard between me and Stanley the last time you were here, but when I went to your camper the next day, you were gone."

"I didn't want to be there when you broke the news to all those people who really believed in you." He looked over at me. "I asked my dad about you to see if he'd tell me you left. But he said that Happy Trails was thriving and you were doing a bang-up job with the place. Even boosting the economy." He reached into the backpack he'd thrown on the floorboard. "I got my copy of *National Parks of America* magazine and about died when I saw your article."

"Oh, gosh. I really underestimated how many people were going to see that." Immediately, I thought of Bobby Ray.

"It goes out to all the national parks. It's a big deal." His words were kind, and I could feel the tension thawing between us. "I guess I jumped the gun and didn't let you explain. I'm sorry for that..." His voice trailed off.

"No problem. I figured you'd be back one day to visit." There was a silence between us the rest of the way, and I couldn't help but wonder about what he was thinking. It was one of those penny-for-your-thoughts moments.

Then I imagined him saying something about how he'd thought about that last time he'd seen me and how things might've turned out differently. But in reality, he was probably worried about his dad.

The sound of light snoring drifted my way. Evidently, he wasn't thinking anything.

A couple of hours later, Ty still asleep, I pulled up to Tammy Jo's house. I quietly clicked the van door closed because I didn't want to wake him. The airplane ride from California to Kentucky was a long one, and I was sure he didn't sleep much on the plane with the concern for his father and brothers on his mind. Not to mention the change in his lifestyle.

The door to the house was cracked opened.

"Hello?" I called but was only greeted by the echo of my voice. "Tammy Jo? It's Mae West. I'm here to pick up the cleaning check for Betts Hager!" I yelled a little louder.

"Out here," Tammy Jo finally called back. "Outside on the balcony."

I walked through the house and out the door from the family room I'd cleaned. She was standing on the porch with Fifi in her arms. Again, the pooch wiggled and jiggled until Tammy Jo finally let her down.

"I didn't open your front door when I yelled for you." I wanted her to know that I didn't just let myself in. "The door was cracked."

The little poodle scurried over to me, jumping up and down for me to pick her up. I did, just in case Tammy Jo decided to give me a tip on the merits of her dog liking me.

Tammy Jo dramatically swept across the balcony, the sheer pink housecoat with fuzzy fur lining floating behind her. She was holding a napkin on her arm. There were two glasses of wine and a cheese plate on the table. It must've been another woman there because there was lipstick on both glasses. Clearly, the bright-red lipstick matched the lipstick on Tammy Jo's mouth. But who wore the orange? That was a bold lipstick color. Something that would stick out.

"Did I interrupt you?" I gazed over at the table.

"No. It's just me." She headed to the door, continuing to blot the napkin on her arm. "Fifi just had her hair clipped, and her nails are so sharp. She scratched me—by accident, of course—when I picked her up."

"Do you want me to look at it?" I asked.

"No. No. I'll be fine. Follow me to Harrison's office. That's where I keep the checks." She walked through the open deck doors. Some stray feathers from her housecoat floated behind her.

"Harrison?" I didn't know who that was.

"My deceased husband." She stopped in her tracks on the way down the hallway. "I guess that's something you and I have in common."

She put her hand on the doorknob of the closed door.

"I guess you checked up on me." I pinched a fake smile, thinking only of a tip.

"Hank told me who you were after you pushed the little cleaning cart around the house that morning." She turned the knob. "I think it's admirable how you're working to pay off your husband's mistakes and misdeeds."

"Ex," I said through an exhausted sigh.

She opened the door and took a couple of steps in before she flipped on the light and let out a bloodcurdling scream before fainting.

Camille Braun was sitting behind Harrison's desk in his big leather chair with a knife stuck in her chest, her eyes wide open.

CHAPTER EIGHT

"Tammy!" I kneeled down, figuring I'd save the one who still had a heartbeat because, by the looks of things, the nanny did not. I put a hand on each of Tammy's shoulders and shook her, trying to get her to come to.

There was no waking up this gal. I pulled my phone out of my back pocket and scrolled through the contacts until I got to Detective Hank Sharp. I sucked in a deep breath before hitting the green call button.

"What in the world could Mae West want with me?" was how Hank answered the phone.

"Hank, there's been a murder." I resisted the urge to say something very sarcastic and decided it was best just to blurt out what happened. "I'm at Tammy Jo Bentley's, picking up my check."

"Mae?" Ty Randal called out through the house. "Are you okay? I heard a scream."

"Back here, Ty!" I yelled toward the hall.

"Ty? What? Mae?" Hank's voice echoed out of the phone.

"Hank, just come to Tammy Jo Bentley's house. There's been a murder." I clicked off the phone and hoped he'd come quickly. I took another look at Tammy Jo before I stood up, guessing she'd be okay while I got Ty.

"Mae, what's wrong?" Ty came down the hall.

My chest heaved up and down. I could feel the tears starting. I curled my lips together. He hurried down the hall and stopped, looking down at me.

"Mae? What's wrong?" His eyes darted across my face.

"The dog nanny." I pointed into the room. "She's…" I looked down and found the courage to look back up at him. "She's been murdered," I said, my voice trailing off.

He dashed past me and into the room. When I turned to go back into the room, I could hear sirens, and Ty was bent over Tammy Jo.

"Tammy?" He looked back at me.

"She passed out." I blinked a few times and reality started to sink in.

He stood up and twisted around. He pointed to the bar.

"Grab a water and a towel," he instructed me.

"What's going on here?" Norman Pettleman stood at the door of the office. He looked around the room, and when he saw Camille in the chair, he turned white. Then his eyes floated down to Tammy Jo. "Tammy!" he gasped, dropping the briefcase from his grip and rushing to Ty.

"Mae, water," Ty told me again.

"Okay." I felt like a robot and like I was having some out-of-body experience. I grabbed the water and unscrewed the top, dousing the towel on my way over to Ty.

Ty took the towel and gently patted Tammy's face with it. Norman held her hand in his and stroked it. The sound of footsteps thundered through the house.

"Police! Come out with your hands up!" Hank's voice was deep and boisterous.

Ty and I looked at each other. He shrugged, and we walked out the door with our hands up. The police officers with Hank ran over to us with their guns drawn, pointing directly at our chests. One took Ty by the shoulder, and one jerked me by the arm. The third officer ran into the office where Tammy and Camille's body were.

"What happened?" Hank looked at me, ignoring Ty.

Detective Elmo Burke, Hank's partner, entered the crime scene. He had the same black suit, round glasses, and shiny bald spot on the top of his head that I remembered from the first time I'd met him.

Ty started to talk. "Listen, man. I just—"

"I'm not talking to you, Randal." Hank put his hand up. "Mae, you called me. What happened?"

"Sir, there's two bodies." The officer stuck his head out the door of the office. "And we can't get the other man to let go of the lady on the ground."

"Tammy Jo Bentley isn't dead. She passed out." Somehow, I was able to get the words out. "Norman is her—"

"I know who Norman is. You stay here," he instructed me. He looked at the officer who still had me by the arms. "You, come with me."

"What about me?" Ty questioned, but Hank ignored him. "Jerk," Ty muttered when he didn't get a response.

The sound of car doors shutting and feet pounding up the front steps of the house caused me to look back down the hall.

Queenie and Dottie ran in. They both had on spandex, tank tops, headbands, and leggings. Queenie looked like a big sun in yellow, and Dottie was wearing light blue.

"What's going on?" Dottie saw Ty and then glanced down the hall at me. "Mae!" She rushed toward me.

"Ma'am, you need to stay right there. This is a crime scene." The officer who had Ty by the arm had let go and made a barrier between Ty and Dottie.

Norman Pettleman had been led out of the room and was seated on the hall floor with his back against the wall. The officer was saying something to him, and Norman just kept nodding with a blank look on his face.

"How did you know I was here?" I asked her.

"Police scanner. Queenie and I were getting ready to go to her Jazzercise Dance Mix class, and she was picking me up when I heard it come over the scanner." That would explain their outfits.

"Mae!" Hank Sharp called my name and looked out the door of the office. His brows rose an inch when he saw Dottie and Queenie. "Can I talk to you in here?"

"Sure." I nodded real fast and went back into the room, keeping my eyes off of that chair. The officer had Tammy sitting up. Next to her was a small vial that looked to be smelling salts.

"Can you tell me what happened here?" he asked. He'd already put white gloves on his hands and a pair of booties over his shoes. So had the other officer.

"I-I..." My voice quivered. My body started to shake a little.

"Are you okay?" Hank snapped the gloves off his hands. He ran his warm hand down my arm and turned me toward him, using his finger to lift my chin to meet his eyes. "Look at me." His words were soft, almost comforting. "Are you okay?" he asked with sincerity.

I licked my lips and sucked in a deep breath. Looking only at him helped me find my voice.

"I cleaned here yesterday for Betts Hager. I forgot to get the check for Betts and told her that I'd stop by for the check after I picked Ty up from the airport." I looked over at Tammy Jo when I heard her sobbing. The officer was trying his best to talk to her, but she was getting louder and louder as the seconds ticked past.

"Mae, what can you tell me about what happened here?" he asked.

"She told me to follow her to the office. Harrison's office." I tried to recall every step.

"Tammy told you or the nanny?" he asked.

"I'm sorry," I apologized. "Tammy asked me to come to the office because that's where the checkbook was. When we opened the door, she flipped on the light, and that's when we saw Camille. Tammy Jo fainted, and I called you."

"Ty?" he asked.

"He came running into the house when he heard Tammy scream." Out of the corner of my eye, I could see the county coroner walking in and heading straight to the body.

"Did you touch anything?" Hank asked, still in a soft voice as if he were talking to a child.

"No. Yes. No." I shook my head and looked over at the coroner as she started to look over the nanny's body.

"Which is it?" he asked and touched my arm again, making me look at him. "Just keep looking at me."

"Ty came in, and he saw that Tammy Jo had fainted, or I told him that or something." It was a little fuzzy to me. "He told me to grab a water bottle and towel from the bar so we could put it on Tammy."

"That's all you touched?" he asked with an expression of relief on his face.

"That's all." I nodded.

"You did good calling me." He offered a smile. "I want you to go on home, and I'll either stop by later or have you come down to the station to give a recorded statement."

"Why would someone kill her?" I asked.

"That's a good question. I don't know yet. You weren't the first person to call about the murder. Someone called it in anonymously, saying that a loud scream had come from Tammy Jo's house. It was ten minutes before you called, and I was already on my way." He pulled his shoulders back when the officer came over and whispered something about the nanny not being dead for long. "You can join the others outside and send in Ty."

"Okay." I looked back at the coroner. She was staring back at me.

Ty had joined Dottie and Queenie in the foyer of the house. The officer had taken yellow crime scene tape and strung it across the beginning of the hall. I ducked under it and walked over to them.

"Are you okay?" Ty asked.

"I'm fine. Hank wants to talk to you now." I pinched a smile that faltered a little at the corners. Once again, I got Ty tangled up in a mess.

This wasn't the first time. Last time he was in town, I practically accused him of killing my ex.

"Mmmmmm-mmmm." Queenie's lips were pressed together. "He's all man." She watched Ty walk down the hall.

"His dad's not bad either," Dottie replied.

"You two, stop it. Someone is dead," I whispered and tugged on them to follow me outside.

"What happened?" Dottie asked and patted her hands to her chest, before taking out a cigarette.

"What is that?" Queenie snarled. "You're supposed to be quitting, and we were going to Jazzercise." Queenie's voice got louder. "Were you going to take a puff between jazz hands?"

"Shush your mouth. I'm nervous." She found a lighter in there too.

I wasn't going to argue with either of them. My head was too busy trying to wrap around what'd happened in the last hour or so that we'd been there. It could've been longer, but I'd lost track of time.

"Go on, Mae," Dottie said, encouraging me. "What happened?"

"Tammy Jo and I found the dog nanny with a knife in her chest. That's it. She's clearly dead, but I did hear the officer tell Hank that she'd not been dead long." I tried to recall if I'd seen something when I'd driven up, but there wasn't anything I could remember that was out of the ordinary.

"This is awful. Are you sure it was murder?" Queenie asked.

"Nah," Dottie said with a hint of sarcasm. "The nanny went into the office and shoved a knife into her own chest."

"Who would do that to her?"

Queenie and Dottie asked all sorts of unanswerable questions as they bantered back and forth until they decided they'd seen enough.

"I guess this will be the talk of the town." Queenie nudged Dottie. "Now that I missed teaching my class, do you want to go back to the Laundry Club for a cup of coffee?"

"I am guessing we should. In case someone comes in to ask us about this." Dottie gave a slight gesture to Tammy Jo's house.

It wasn't too long after they left that Ty came back out.

"What did Hank say?" I asked a flustered Ty.

"He's just a jerk. He wanted to know why I was in town and how long I was staying. Nothing that had to do with this." He walked toward the minivan. "Are you coming?"

"Yeah. I mean, I guess we can go." I reached into my pocket for the keys.

"Do you want me to drive? You seem a little unsteady still." He'd noticed I was trying to keep my hands from shaking.

Without even saying a word, I handed him the keys. He opened the passenger door for me and took my elbow to help me into the van. He shut the door, and Hank Sharp was staring at me from the front door.

As if dealing with seeing a dead body wasn't enough, the chill between Ty and Hank was impossible to ignore.

Ty started the van and put it into gear, stepping on the gas pedal. We didn't say a word. On the way down the driveway, I noticed the gardener was mowing the pasture.

"Slow down!" Ty yelled, jerking the wheel as a car barreled down the driveway, almost hitting us. For just a second, I saw the person driving the car. It was Ava Cox.

"What on earth is she doing here?" I had a death grip on the door handle while Ty fought to keep the van on the driveway.

"She's going to kill someone." He steadied the wheel then stopped the van, looking in the rearview mirror. "Who was that?"

"That was Ava Cox." I turned completely around in my seat to look out the back windows.

"Related to Grady and Junior?" Ty remembered that my now-deceased ex-husband's killer was Grady Cox, Jr., the son of Ava and Grady Cox, who were victims of Paul's Ponzi scheme.

"The one and only wife and mother..." My voice trailed off as I slowly turned around.

"I wonder why she's going to see Tammy Jo Bentley?" He asked a very good question that set my curiosity on high alert.

"I don't know, but I want to." I let out a deep sigh of relief as I felt calmness sweep over me once Ty had the van heading straight to town and away from the Bentley house.

CHAPTER NINE

Ty and I didn't have much to say after we left Tammy Jo's. I was too busy wondering who in the world would kill Camille.

"Poor Tammy Jo," I finally said after Ty had pulled into the parking lot of the hospital where his dad would be discharged from about now.

"I can't believe it. Was anyone else in the house when you got there?" He turned off the ignition and put the keys on the middle console.

"No. She said it was just her." I snapped my fingers. "There were two glasses of wine and a cheese plate on the deck where she was standing." It was a little tidbit I'd forgotten to tell Hank.

"And what does that prove?" Ty asked.

"Maybe whoever she was eating with went into the house and killed the nanny." It didn't sound that farfetched.

Ty laughed.

"What?" I asked. "You asked me if anyone else was there. Obviously, there was." I shrugged.

"I'm not laughing at that. I'm laughing because there was so much excitement in your voice when you pulled this theory out of the air. It's like you're passionate about this. That's all." He unlocked the doors and put his hand on the handle. "Thanks for picking me up." Slowly, his head turned toward me. "I'm also sorry that I didn't get the opportunity to say goodbye before I left. I'd like to make it up to you and take you to supper sometime. And not a campground supper."

"You mean like a real restaurant or the Normal Diner?" I asked, knowing that more than likely he was going to go back to work there. Especially now that his dad had been hurt.

"That's exactly what I mean. I'd like to make it up to you," he said in a soft tone.

"Are you taking me on a date?" I teased and narrowed my eyes. "Or are you trying to get out of paying for any extras at the campground?"

"Yep. That's it. You got me." He winked and got out of the car, leaving me hanging on his every word.

I tried to stop the huge smile on my face and clumsily climbed over the console of the van, nearly falling face-first into the dash. When I finally got situated in the driver's seat, I looked out of the windshield. Ty had watched me maneuver to the driver's seat and was standing in front of the hospital, looking at me and shaking his head.

On the way back to the campground, I tried like heck to remember things about Tammy Jo's house and what'd happened, but all my thoughts were about Ty. I even looked at my phone a few times to see if he'd already texted me.

There wasn't a cloud in the sky. It was bright blue with the sun beaming down on the town. The campground had only a slight breeze due to all the big trees that shielded it. Though it was smoldering hot, it would be gorgeous on the hiking trails of the Daniel Boone National Forest.

The campground was starting to look like a desert. Literally. Dottie had gone overboard with the theme. She had blow-up cactuses tied down around the lake. She'd turned the tiki bar into a desert bar by scattering cowboy boots and a few sombreros around. These parties had become very popular, and it was nice that the campers had the opportunity to get to know each other.

I'd learned that part of the camping community was learning where everyone was from. A few of the campers had made plans to travel to each other's states and meet up at different parks around the country. I especially loved hearing about favorite national parks and locations. It was a fun atmosphere, and I was honored to be part of it.

I pulled the van around the lake and saw Henry and Bobby Ray talking to a few guests.

"Howdy," Henry greeted me.

"Hey." I motioned for him to come to the open window. "Do you mind jumping in and giving me a hand with Ty's bags."

"Bags?" Henry poked his head into the van. "What's up with all that?"

"Before I dropped him off at the hospital, he said that he was moving back and brought some stuff with him." I left out the part about the murder and the fact Ty'd asked me out.

"I'll be back," Henry told the group he was talking to before getting in. "So, did y'all reconnect that little spark between you?"

"Spark?" I laughed. "I don't think so."

"Mmhhh, there was no denying the spark you two had going the night before he left." Henry knew everything about this campground and everyone in it. "But if you don't want to tell me, that's fine. I've got eyes."

When we got to Ty's camper, I parked the car and got out without saying a word, letting Henry rely on his eyes.

I used the key I had and unlocked the camper while Henry grabbed a couple of the bags.

"Don't mess with those," Henry said when I went back to the van to grab a bag.

"I'm good. I can help." It sounded like I really wanted to help, but I really just wanted to touch Ty's suitcase.

"Here." Henry took the bag from me, just as my phone rang in my back pocket. "You go on and get done what you need to get done. I've got this."

"Okay. Fine." I gave in, knowing that Henry was too much of a gentleman to let me even take one step carrying something. "Ava Cox," I whispered, reading the name scrolling across my phone. "Henry, you have this?" I hit the answer button when he nodded and gestured for me to go on. "Hello?"

I got into the van and put it in gear, turning the wheel back toward my camper.

"Mae, this is Ava Cox. I know I'm the last person you thought you'd ever hear from, but I need to talk to you right now." She left no room for protest. "I'm on my way over to Happy Trails, and I'd like a cup of coffee. The detective said you had a nice coffeemaker."

"Ava?" I pulled the phone from my ear when I noticed it went silent. "She hung up on me," I said and pulled onto the concrete pad next to my camper.

Before I got out of the car, I sent Betts Hager a text, telling her I'd yet been able to go to the nursing home to clean the two apartments there, but I'd do them this afternoon, with a follow-up text to let her know that we'd meet up and exchange cars after that. Now that Ty was back, Betts was free from babysitting his brothers and should be able to resume her cleaning schedule.

After I filled the coffeepot's carafe with water and scooped coffee into the basket, I quickly pulled my unruly hair into a ponytail and changed my clothes into a pair of shorts and tank top. It was way too hot to try to look cute, especially when I was just going to clean up after a couple little old ladies. I did have my eye on a cute jumper to pull on after I finished at the nursing home, in case I had a visitor. Like Ty.

The coffeepot beeped to tell me that the brewing cycle was complete while I splashed water on my face. My eyes were closed as the cold water hit my face. They jerked open when the image of Camille's eyes staring blankly back at me with the knife in her chest popped into my head. I stood in front of the mirror, staring back at myself with the towel over my mouth. There was a knock at the door, and I swiped the towel across my face.

I stuck my head out the bathroom door and hollered, "Come in."

"It's me, Ava," she called, and I heard the door click closed.

Quickly, I put one pump of sunscreen in my hands and applied it to my face before I went out to greet her.

"I have to say I was shocked to see you at Tammy Jo Bentley's house, and now you're here." I took down two mugs from the hooks that were hanging from the cabinet next to the sink. It was all about space conservation when you lived in a trailer. When I was going through the renovation, I knew I wanted to have a little cozy cottage feel.

"This is charming." Ava looked around. She held up two fingers. "Two teaspoons of sugar." Her petite frame looked smaller since the last time I'd seen her. Her long curly black hair was pulled back at the nape of her neck. She still had perfect million-dollar olive skin.

I got the creamer out of the small refrigerator and the sugar packets out of the cabinet, giving them to her so she could doctor up her own coffee. I took mine black, and it smelled so good. I was looking out the window over the kitchen sink when I heard a car engine.

"Is your car running?" I asked.

"Yes. I don't plan on being here long." She took the coffee mug. "Let's just get down to it. There's no sense in making small talk when there's business to be had."

Ava stirred the coffee and set the spoon on the table. She had a briefcase with her. She placed it on the table and rummaged through the contents. I sat in the chair across from her. Finally, she took out a page from a legal pad.

"I'm Tammy Jo Bentley's lawyer." She looked up at me with high brows. "She has been taken into custody for the murder of Camille."

"Really?" I questioned.

"Yes. I don't think she did it, and I need you as a witness." She rolled her shoulders back. Her jaw tensed. "I'm not going to sit here and say that it's easy looking at you since your husband is the reason my son is in jail and my husband is dead."

"Ex," I reminded her, but bit my tongue about how her husband and my ex had been best friends for years. Her husband did give my ex the millions of dollars Ava and Grady had built up from their horse business, but my ex didn't make her son, Grady Jr., kill her husband or my ex. That was all on him.

"Still, I do have to commend you for making an effort to fix his mess by paying people back and bringing the campground back to life, which helps the economy." She tapped her pen on the pad of paper. "Anyways,

I want to know a good time for us to meet so we can discuss today and previous days you've been with my client."

"I can pretty much make up my own schedule. But I'm not sure I have a lot to add. I don't really know Tammy Jo. I just cleaned for her one time for a friend." I took a drink of the coffee.

"Really?" She put the pen down and gave me a strange look. She threw the pad and pen back into her briefcase. She stood up. "Can you come with me?"

"Sure." I stood up and followed her out to her car.

She opened the front door, stuck her briefcase on her seat, and then opened the back door. She pulled out Fifi.

"Here." She pushed the dog into my chest, and out of reflex, I took her. "For someone who is just an acquaintance, Tammy Jo seemed pretty confident that you could watch after her prize-winning dog."

"Me?" I adjusted Fifi so her nails wouldn't tear me up like they'd done to Tammy Jo's arm. "I don't think so." Firmly, I held the dog out for Ava to take.

"She doesn't have anyone else." She shrugged and slammed the back door.

"Nope. She's got the gardener—and what about that insurance guy, Norman?" I asked.

"Those are all people who work for her." She opened the driver's side door, not listening to my protest. "Not trusted individuals."

"Umm, no. I can't take care of a dog. Especially a dog that looks like this." I turned Fifi toward me to look at her, and her long tongue slapped against my cheek. "You! You can keep her. Tammy Jo is your client, and you must be a trusted individual in her life."

"Don't be ridiculous." Ava wasn't going to take the dog.

"I don't have a dog bed, food, or anything else. She's an award-winning dog from what I hear." I rolled my eyes. "That sort of class is not found here at Happy Trails. I don't have a fancy watch to train her nor do I have the time to put her down for her daily naps, much less play with her."

"I'm sure she'll be fine with a few days off of her vigorous schedule."

Ava wasn't leaving any room for me to wiggle out of this. "I almost forgot." Ava got back out of the car and opened the trunk. She took out a pink, bedazzled bag with Fifi's name embroidered on the front in white thread. "Everything you need. Now, I've got to get going. I have to go to the police station to talk to my client."

What was going on here? I was at a loss for words. I stood there stunned and unable to say anything, not even noticing Ty and his brothers driving past in Ron Randal's car.

Fifi continued to lick my face. I continued to watch Ava's taillights until they turned out of the campground.

"Did you get a dog?" Ty's younger brother, Timmy, ran up to me and took Fifi right out of my arms. "Can I play with her?"

I still couldn't bring myself to say anything. What was Tammy Jo thinking? Why me? I had to go see her, but I had to get those apartments at the nursing home cleaned too.

"I'm babysitting." The strange words came out of my mouth as Ty walked up to me.

"Wasn't that the car that practically killed us today?" Ty asked, watching Timmy play with Fifi. Sean kept his distance. Fifi yipped and barked, jumping around and biting at the hem of Timmy's shorts.

"Yes. She's a lawyer, and Tammy Jo has been taken into custody for the murder of Camille Braun."

"I thought you said you didn't know Tammy Jo until yesterday," Ty said.

"I didn't. For some reason, she wants me to keep her dog until she gets out of jail." I picked up the bag. "Ava wouldn't let me decline. She just hopped in her car and took off. Just like that."

"Nice bag." Ty laughed. "Pink might be your color."

"Hush." I nudged him with my elbow. "I need a favor." I gnawed on the edge of my lip. Like he didn't already have enough on his plate.

"I'm worried about what it might be." He gave me the side-eye.

"I told Betts I'd clean a few apartments at the nursing home too. I've still got to do those, and I know she doesn't have your brothers, but I'm sure she's so tired from keeping them busy." I pointed to the dog. "I still want to clean for her, but I can't take Fifi with me."

"Huuuh... un." His jaw dropped, and he wagged a finger at me. "No way."

"Look. Your brother loves her, and it'll only be like an hour. It's a nursing home apartment." I reminded him how small those were. "An hour, tops."

He looked at his brother and then back at me a couple of times. I had my lips turned down in a frown with my hands together, batting my eyelashes.

"Fine. More than an hour, and we bring her there." He finally gave in.

"Thank you!" I threw my arms around his neck.

"I could get used to this," he whispered, sending goosebumps down my spine.

CHAPTER TEN

Many times, I have let my mind wonder what was going to happen to me when I got older. There were so many stories about how expensive nursing homes were. When I married Paul, I thought my golden years would be taken care of. Walking into the senior living area of the nursing home made me sad. There was a real fear that I wasn't going to have anyone to take care of me or see to my needs.

Tilly Blake and Olga Watson didn't seem to worry about anyone but the two of them.

"I've seen you here a time or two." Tilly Blake had dyed black hair down to her shoulders. There was a small scar on her right eyebrow, and her two front teeth were crooked. She was only five feet in height but had a mighty boisterous voice.

"I've seen her at church." Olga Watson's black hair was cut to below her earlobes. She didn't have on makeup like Tilly. By her appearance, Olga didn't get ready in front of a mirror. She was somewhat disheveled compared to Tilly. She stood about five feet seven and had a little more girth than Tilly.

They bantered back and forth about which one saw me first before they finally let me in the door of Tilly's apartment.

"You know that we don't really have Betts clean too much, right?" Tilly asked.

"I understand that you love to watch *Wheel of Fortune*." I looked at the two best friends, thinking it must be really nice to have good friends at their age.

"We do love Vanna. She's a snappy dresser." Olga nodded to Tilly for confirmation and Tilly ho-hummed.

"Get in here before the first spin." Tilly and Olga walked ahead of me.

"I think it's great the two of you are best friends." I got all the trash in the kitchen like Betts had said to do while they told me how they'd become friends.

"We both protested coming here." Tilly and Olga talked over each other. "We got here the same day. Both of us spitting vinegar."

While they talked, I cleaned the kitchen sink, wiped down the counters, and quickly mopped the small kitchen floor when I noticed there were some spills that'd not been fully cleaned up.

"After we found each other, we realized we liked the same things. Gossip being one of them." Olga was sitting on the couch, and Tilly was sitting in a big, puffy recliner.

"Everyone likes a good tale," I said on my way to the bathroom.

"Have you heard about anything new?" I heard one of them ask me while I emptied the trashcan in the bathroom and sprayed cleaner in the toilet.

"Nope. Not a thing," I said loud enough for them to hear me and used the toilet brush to clean the inside of the bowl. There was some silence as I busied myself cleaning the sink, counter, and tub.

The tick of the wheel spinning on the TV show reminded me of the pocket watch. I almost told them the gossip about the watch being worth 2.2 million dollars but decided that I didn't want to get into how I knew about it.

"Did you see Ron Randal is back in rehab?" Olga said to Tilly.

"Why this time?" Tilly asked Olga.

"I don't know."

"That is something I do know," I said after I'd returned to the living room. I combined all the trash into one bag and gathered all the cleaning supplies back into the bucket.

"Sit on down and give us the scoop." Olga patted the seat next to her.

For the next half hour, I told them about Ron and how I ran the campground, knowing that, before I left there, I'd made two new friends that I'd found out were in their eighties. I couldn't help but smile the whole way home, thinking that friends come in all ages.

I grabbed a quick shower before I went to Ty's to get Fifi. He was trying to get Timmy calmed down. Sean was playing video games. Ty was busy with his family, so I left with Fifi.

Daydreaming about Ty Randal being a few campers away was better than any sleeping medication when I couldn't get images of Camille Braun's creepy wide-eyed face out of my head. I'd like to say the sun shining through the window or chirping birds woke me up from a nice dream about Ty, but it was a white fluff ball, yipping and scratching on the metal camper door, which sounded like nails on a chalkboard.

"Fifi, go to bed." I dragged the pillow back over my head after I looked at my digital clock. The blue LED bulbs read five o' clock. My muscles were aching from all the bending down and cleaning I'd been doing.

I could have slept a few more hours, but Fifi continued to yip and scratch on the metal door, sending my nerves on high alert. Since my bedroom was located in the back of the camper, I'd gotten the idea to let her act up, and I'd closed the bedroom door, but when she started whining, I knew the poor thing meant business.

"Alright." I threw the covers back and grabbed a Happy Trails Campground sweatshirt on my way to the front of the camper.

Dottie had insisted we sell tchotchkes with the Happy Trails logo on them in the office. I was glad she had insisted because I'd been pleasantly surprised at how many people liked to collect and purchase items from the campgrounds they visited across the US.

I dug through Fifi's bag to get her leash. There was still a lack of trust between me and her. I wasn't sure she'd even listen to me.

According to the directions in her bag, she knew a lot of commands, started her day around this awful morning hour, and ate her special diet food, which was in my refrigerator, after her morning walk.

"Come on, Fifi." I clipped the pink leash onto her diamond-encrusted collar before picking her up.

The door creaked when I opened it, and the two metal steps to the ground groaned under my bare feet. Fifi darted straight ahead when I put her on the ground. She stopped as soon as the leash went taut. The moon was still hanging high in the sky with the stars bright and gathered around it. Lightning bugs fluttered about, dotting the darkness with little drops of blinking light. The lake looked so pretty with their lights reflecting off the calm water. The humidity was thick, and with the stars out, I knew that it wasn't going to rain. This was a good thing since Dottie had worked so hard on the Summer Sizzler party.

The sudden realization Fifi was here due to a dead body and Tammy Jo Bentley being in jail on a murder charge made my heart heavy. Tammy Jo taking me into the office where Camille had been killed didn't make sense. If she had killed her, why would she take me to the office and why would she faint?

It wasn't a fake faint either. She was out cold.

"Someone is in deep thought." Ty's voice broke through the chirping crickets and the bullfrogs.

"Ty, what on earth are you doing out here?" I asked, knowing that I wouldn't be here if it weren't for Fifi.

I tugged on the leash a little more so Fifi would follow me. Ty's camper wasn't next to mine, but he was just a couple of lots down from me.

"I can't sleep. The dog nanny is on my mind," he said.

As he got closer, the darkness disappeared around him, exposing a shirtless and muscular Ty.

"Aren't you burning up in that sweatshirt?" he asked.

"Not me." About right now I was liking the fact the sweatshirt was covering up the goosebumps trailing along my arms. "What about Camille?" I asked, curious to know if we were thinking the same thing.

"While you were cleaning at the nursing home last night, I watched my brothers playing with Fifi. I kept thinking about what Tammy Jo's possible reason for murdering someone who took such great care of Fifi could be. I mean, it doesn't make sense," he said, making a good point.

Fifi continued to walk on the road that led around the campground, going toward Ty's camper and near the bungalows at the very back of Happy Trails. Ty and I let her lead the way, stopping when she stopped to smell or do her business.

"That's not the only thing that doesn't make sense. Hank said he was on his way to Tammy Jo's when I called because someone had called it in anonymously. Plus, why would she take me into the office if she did kill Camille?" I asked. "And she fainted!"

"Yeah. She wouldn't have fainted if she'd known because it wouldn't have shocked her like that." Ty was right.

"So, what now?" I asked.

"What do you mean?" He stopped in front of his camper.

"Tammy Jo is accused of murder and in jail. Fifi doesn't want to live in a campground. I can't keep her." I shrugged.

"Oh, no." He wagged a finger in front of me. "You aren't going to stick your nose in this one. I'm certainly not."

"I don't think it would hurt to look into things. You know, the front door was cracked when I went to her door." It was a minor detail that I'd forgotten and should probably tell Hank. My jaw dropped.

"What? I don't like that look on your face." Ty's eyebrows furrowed. "It's telling me that you're thinking way too much about this."

"I completely forgot that when I walked into the house, I called out for Tammy Jo. She was on the back porch. There were two wineglasses. Both had lipstick on them. Was one Camille's? Did something go wrong and she really did kill Camille?" I started to ramble about these conspiracy theories. "I mean, she said I'd not interrupted anything. Then there was the gardener and Camille. Camille was upset after they had this hushed conversation while I was there cleaning. And Tammy Jo had scratches on her arm."

"Whoa. Whoa," Ty whispered and looked around. "What was all that?"

"I need coffee." I gnawed on the edge of my lip. I had an itching to write all of this down before I forget. "Come on, Fifi."

She was resistant to the gentle tug from the leash. From the note, Fifi wasn't used to a leash hooked on her collar; she wore a harness around her chest that had a place for the leash to clip to. When I held up the harness, I couldn't tell which strap went where, so that's why I fastened it to her collar.

"Let me grab a shirt and check on the boys, and I'll be right down." Ty headed in the direction of his camper.

"Let's go, Fifi." I continued to think about the gardener on my way back. I needed to recall everything they'd talked about.

I turned on all the lights in the camper and got out Fifi's food. The smell was enough to gag me, and there was no way poor Fifi liked it. I set the container on the ground instead of dividing up the portions. Just as I imagined, Fifi walked up to it, smelled it, and turned her nose up at it.

"I don't blame you." I picked up the container and put the lid back on before tossing it into the trash. I'd worry about the repercussions of that later. I opened the refrigerator and took out some leftovers. There were hot dogs, chicken, spaghetti, and some rice.

"I know you probably shouldn't eat hot dogs, but I think you might like chicken and rice." I talked to her like she understood me.

Her white pom-pom ears perked up like she understood. Her furless tail wagged.

"That's a yes to me." I grabbed a paper plate from one of the cabinets and put a little of the chicken and rice on it just to see if she liked it.

I set it on the ground in front of her to let her sniff it while I got the coffee ready. Before I could even get the eight scoops of coffee into the filter, Fifi had scarfed down all of the food.

"You must be really hungry." I pondered whether I should give her more. She must've known what I was thinking because she barked, turned in a circle, and wagged her tail. "I'll give you more."

I picked up the paper plate, hit the brew button on the coffee pot, and got more chicken and rice out of the refrigerator.

Fifi was busy eating the rest of her breakfast when I went into the bathroom to brush my teeth and get a little more presentable for Ty. The sight of my frizzy hair in the mirror made me groan. Ty had seen exactly what I looked like when I woke up, and it wasn't pleasant. I wouldn't say I'm a pretty girl, but I could hold my own. I wasn't the thinnest, and I had curves in the right places. I was a little more on the regular size. By today's modeling standards, I'd be considered plus-size. The size of my hair didn't make it better.

I ran a brush through my hair and pulled it into a messy bun on top of my head. That was one good thing about having long hair. My curls did have some weight to them, pulling them into long curls and not tight to the head like they would be if my hair was shoulder-length. Still, the humidity did nothing to make it any better.

The dark roast coffee smelled so good and filled the entire inside of the camper. There was a knock on the door, and I heard it open.

"Mae?" Ty called and then quickly greeted Fifi. "Hey, pretty girl."

It was funny how his voice changed to a high-pitch squeak when he talked to her. I guess most people did that to dogs.

"I'm changing." I called from the bedroom and grabbed a pair of shorts and a T-shirt out of my drawer.

"I'm going to make us a cup of coffee." Ty made himself at home. I smiled to myself.

"Thanks." I walked down the hall to find him pouring the cups. I got a pad of paper and a pen from the one of the kitchen drawers. I put them on the table. "I think we need to write down everything we know."

"And why would we do that?" He looked at me over the top of his mug as he took a sip.

"Because of Fifi. She's not happy here and the quicker Tammy Jo gets out, the better." I took the cup he made for me and sat down in one of the chairs at the table.

"She looks pretty happy to me." He smiled.

Fifi had licked her plate clean and happily chewed on a pink poodle stuffed animal. When she looked up at me, our eyes met and she wagged her tail, throwing the stuffed animal in the air.

"Show off," I laughed. "She does look pretty happy."

"Right. If she had a nanny and this strict of a schedule, she couldn't be a dog." He picked up the list from her that I'd put on the table. "I mean, you have to make sure she gets these vitamins for premium breeding?"

"Does it say that on there?" I admit I didn't really read through the note. "You should've smelled the dog food they want me to give her. I couldn't give it to her. She loved the chicken and rice."

"Oh, Mae. If Tammy Jo does get out of jail, she might go back for killing you for not taking care of that dog." He smiled. His eyes twinkled. I gulped.

"Then we need to get her out of jail before I do any more damage." I dragged the paper and pen toward me. "Now. I think we can write down Tammy Jo's name and the gardener."

"Why the gardener again?" he asked.

"Because when I was cleaning, I saw Camille watch the gardener. Even before that, I saw them huddled together outside. They jerked apart when they saw me coming." I talked and wrote their names down.

"It's not a crime to talk to people you work with. It certainly doesn't scream murder." He was playing the devil's advocate, and I appreciated that. But I ignored him.

"What about my overhearing them arguing about how she couldn't be with him? That Fifi relied on her. Tammy Jo relied on her. Then she came back through the house with her head in her hands. I think she was crying." I wrote "motive" under the gardener's name. "He was rejected by Camille, and he killed her."

"What about Tammy Jo?" he asked.

"I wonder if she and Camille had gotten into an argument. When I got there to clean, Tammy Jo had Fifi. Hank Sharp and Norman Pettleman were there." I wrote down Norman's name. "When you and I went back to get the check for Betts Hager, there were two wineglasses.

Both had lipstick on them. There was the bright red that Tammy Jo apparently wears all the time; the other was orange."

"Orange?" Ty's nose curled.

"Yes. That's a bold color." I snapped my finger. "Do you think it was someone with the Kentucky Kennel Association? I mean…" My voice trailed off. "The suspect list could be endless."

"Mae, I think you are truly getting in over your head now. Your imagination is running wild." He wasn't amused with my theories. "Maybe the mailman killed her."

"Why?" I asked with wide eyes.

"Calm down." He picked up his coffee. "I was kidding. Maybe Fifi did it because she was tired of being bullied by Camille."

"Shut up." I couldn't contain the smile finding its way across my lips. "You think you're funny."

"I'm pretty funny." He winked. "Did you still want to go to dinner tonight?"

"Of course." I looked down at my list because I could feel the red starting to roll up my face in a full blush.

"You look like you've got more writing to do." He stood up. I stood up too. "I've got to go check on the boys before Betts comes over to sit with them while I go to work."

"You're at the diner today?" I asked and looked over at my phone that was still on the charger by the kitchen sink. I was checking to see if Betts had left me a message to clean today.

"I'm going to be there for the breakfast and lunch crowd before coming back here for the Summer Sizzler. Dottie conned me into donating the pig for the roast." He stood at the open camper door. The moon's rays were like a spotlight over his head, making it appear as if he had a halo around him.

Inwardly, I sighed.

"Then I'll see you at the party and for the supper you owe me." I was careful not to say date even though it felt like a date.

He gave a nod and disappeared into the dawn.

"Fifi, you might be going home quicker than you want to," I said to the white furball that'd curled up with her paw resting on the stuffed animal. "You are cute."

There was a slight flutter in my heart. Was her cuteness getting to me? I let out a long sigh, shook my head, sent Betts a quick text about helping out if needed, and refilled my cup with coffee before I headed back to the bathroom to get a shower.

The entire time I got ready, I continued to think about how I could get my hands on any documents to do with the KKA. Maybe someone was there to hurt Fifi, and Camille was in the way. It appeared that nothing was too strange for this dog business.

The phone chirped a text while I put the shorts and T-shirt back on for the day. The day was still going to be a scorcher. My hair would dry naturally, and hopefully, I'd be able to pull it back up in a couple of hours to keep it out of my face. Though I was planning on fixing it before my date... um... supper with Ty tonight.

I checked the text and it was Betts. She said that she hated to ask me, but she was on her way to Ty's to watch the boys, and she always cleaned the police station on Saturday morning at six before they got too busy.

"I figured I'd call you," I said when Betts answered her phone. "I'd love to help, but how do you clean the police department?"

"It's easy," she whispered into the phone. "All the rooms have trash cans; those need to be emptied. I sweep the floors with a broom since they are that nasty old tile stuff. I don't mop this week. That's next week, but I should be back next week."

She continued to tell me things I needed to make sure were done, and I scribbled them down on the pad of paper where I'd written down my thoughts on Camille's murder.

"Are you sure you don't mind?" she asked.

"Not at all." I flipped a couple pieces of paper on the pad back and looked at the list I'd started to make. I needed to talk to Tammy Jo, and this was how it was going to happen.

"Great. Come down here and get the van. It shouldn't take you too long, so you'll be back in plenty of time before the Summer Sizzler," she said.

"No problem. Dottie took this on herself as the new event coordinator of the campground." We had a couple more exchanges before we hung up. I changed again into a T-shirt that I didn't mind getting all dirty along with a different pair of shorts. "Fifi, you be a good girl," I called to her, grabbing my purse on the way out.

"Are you sure you don't mind?" Betts asked as the humidity filled around us. She fanned her hand in front of her face. "I even left a detailed note on what to clean on the passenger seat just in case you said yes."

"Not at all, in fact." I looked around. The dawn had transformed into an orange-and-yellow-tinted sky with the Daniel Boone National Forest poking up. This was one of the reasons I loved living here. This was nature at its finest, and I'd realized how much I'd missed living in the city. "Did you hear about Tammy Jo Bentley's dog nanny, Camille Braun?"

"I did. Poor Lester got the call." She shook her head. She drew her hand up to her mouth. "I forgot you cleaned for me at her house. Did you see anything?"

"I found her when I went to pick up your check, which I still didn't get." I pinched my lips.

"We probably won't get it, but I'll still pay you." Betts looked over her shoulder at the camper. "The boys are asleep, but I have a second. Tell me all about how you found her."

I quickly told her how I picked up Ty, which was met with a giggle of glee that came right from Betts's gut, then I led into how I went to get the check and saw Camille.

"I can't believe this. This is the second time a dead body has found its way into your life since you moved here," she said with dazed exasperation.

"Geesh, tell me about it. You've not heard anything yet." I pointed down to my camper. "Tammy Jo thinks I can keep Fifi for her while she's in jail. Her lawyer dropped her off to me last night."

Betts seemed to really enjoy me keeping Fifi because she let out a laugh as if I'd sincerely amused her.

"Did you know that watch on the mantle is worth 2.2 million dollars?" I asked since I knew she had to dust it on a weekly basis.

"I knew it had to be worth something since it's thought to be the reason Camille was killed," she said, grabbing my attention.

"What?" There was disbelief in my voice. No wonder she said that she'd told me too much when I went to see her in the holding cell. Maybe it was something Hank had known and told her to keep quiet about. I gnawed on the edge of my lip, listening intently to what she had to say.

"Yeah. Didn't you know it's been stolen?" she asked, looking back after a light came on in the camper. "I've got to go. Thanks." She waved me off after exchanging keys, leaving me there with more questions and theories to add to my list.

CHAPTER ELEVEN

"Listen," I said, talking to Fifi like the paper said. I was trying to put a dog diaper on her. "According to this note, you're about to have your monthly girly thing. And this says that you need to wear a pad."

This was something I never would've dreamed I'd say to a dog. Maybe a future daughter, but a dog?

Fifi squirmed and jerked away as I tried to keep her in between my legs to get the hole on top of the diaper around her tail. Once I had that on, I had to get a leg in each leg hole and then Velcro it around her little waist.

"I'm not going to let you win." I was so determined that it brought a sweat to my brow. "There." I patted the Velcro in place and let go. She bounced around the camper, almost walking completely on her front paws with her hiney in the air. I simply shook my head and wondered what on earth Camille enjoyed about her job. "Wait."

My eyes narrowed, and I looked off into the distance as more conspiracy theories rolled around my head. I pushed myself off the floor and sat back in the kitchen chair. Pulling the notebook close to me, I started to write.

"What did the will say about Fifi if Tammy Jo died?" I tapped the pen on the paper. "What if it was Tammy Jo that was supposed to die, not Camille, and someone from the KKA came into the house and thought it was Tammy Jo in the office." I gnawed on the edge of my lip. "Why was Camille in the office? What's in the office?"

Sitting in the camper wasn't going to get these questions answered, nor was it going to get the police station cleaned before the workday started. But, I thought, some of these questions could be answered if I could see Tammy Jo while I was there.

The edges of my lips curled up. It was a brilliant idea. Tammy Jo just might have a morning visitor.

I grabbed my phone and my crossbody purse.

"You be a good girl," I said to Fifi, using my foot to keep her from running out the door. We did a little dance around each other until I finally got out the door and locked it behind me.

The early morning burnt orange sun cast a beautiful glow over the campground and a shadow over Bobby Ray, who was putting quarters in the newspaper machine in front of the recreation center up near the office. He gave a wave with the paper when he noticed it was me, and I waved back. I looked in the rearview mirror. Bobby Ray had folded the paper and stuck it under his armpit on his way back toward the bungalows. His chin was up in the air like he, too, had noticed the gorgeous sunrise. I gripped the wheel and smiled. Never in a million years did I think I'd ever see Bobby Ray Bond again.

I took my time driving up the one-way street when I reached downtown. The shades of dawn were like one of those sand art projects in those crazy blown-glass bottles. Layers upon layers of different yellows and oranges.

The Cookie Crumble Bakery sign flashed OPEN. My mouth watered.

I pulled the van into an empty spot. There was no better place to take donuts to than a police station. It was perfect to sweeten them up and distract them if I did get a chance to sneak in to see Tammy Jo.

"Good morning." The woman behind the counter had a nice and warm smile on her face. Her cheeks were plump and made her eyes squint. "You got here just in time." She walked down the long glass case with rows and rows of different kinds of donuts. "The cinnamon and sugar donuts just came out of the oven. I can't tell you how amazing they are."

"Then I'll get two dozen of those. I'm on my way to clean the police department, and I can't think of anything better to bring them." My eyes glanced over all the different sweet treats.

"You are going to be their favorite person." She plucked a white piece of parchment paper from the box with one hand and grabbed a cardboard box with the other. "Do you own a cleaning business?"

"No. I've been working for my friend, Betts Hager." I tapped the glass. "Can I get a chocolate donut for me?"

"On the house." Her nose curled up, squishing all of her freckles together.

"That's so nice. Thank you." I said, then figured I'd better introduce myself. "I'm Mae West. I own Happy Trails Campground."

"I'm Christine Watson." She looked up and over the counter, setting the box on top before she turned to pluck another piece of parchment out of the box. Brown strands of hair from her ponytail flew out in silky wisps. "My sister and I own the bakery."

"You and your sister are smart people." I pulled out my wallet from the crossbody purse and walked over to the end of the counter.

Christine got my donut and put it in a separate little bag.

"Will that be all?" she asked, rubbing her hands down her waist apron.

"Yes—thanks." I turned when I heard the bell over the door ding someone's arrival.

A few hikers walked in, followed by a couple more. They were wearing hiking shorts, long socks, and hiking boots. Christine rang me up while they browsed, pointing at and discussing which donuts they wanted.

"It's about time for my early morning hikers to get here. I get a couple of waves in here, and it's pretty consistent." She pulled out an iPad with a Square Reader attached to it. "That'll be twelve dollars."

I handed her my debit card, and she swiped it.

"I put a card in there because I'd like to have Betts call me. We've been trying to find someone who can clean for us every night." She handed me another card. "This is for you in case your campground needs any donuts for the office. We'd love to work with you."

"That's really a good idea. I'll give it to the manager who is in charge of all events and social activities." I slipped my debit card and the business card into my crossbody bag. "Thanks again for the donut," I said and left with my treats.

The police station was a little bit outside downtown in the business district right near the Cookie Crumble. The white courthouse was the tallest building and right in the middle with the police station attached to it. The line of police cars told me where exactly it was located.

I scanned the parking lot for the black cars the detectives drove. There was relief in my gut when I didn't notice any, and I prayed Hank was on park duty today. He was not only a detective for the Normal Police Department; he was the park deputy for the Daniel Boone National Forest. I didn't know his schedule, but if he wasn't here, then he couldn't be watching my every move.

There was plenty of parking in front at this time of day. I looked over the list of cleaning supplies Betts had written for me. I needed a broom, mop, and feather duster, along with the cleaning supplies. According to her note, she really only cleaned the offices; there was another service that cleaned the cells, bathrooms, and anything associated with inmates.

I headed through the door with the donuts, having decided I'd start with those. It was as quiet as a church in the station. When you walked in, there was a receptionist window and a door.

"Can I help you?" a petite older woman with soft gray hair and saggy jowls asked after she slid the window open. The nameplate on the other side of the glass had "Agnes" engraved across the brass.

"Hi," I greeted who I assumed to be Agnes and stepped closer to the window. "I'm Mae West, and I'm here to fill in for Betts Hager, ma'am."

That was one thing I didn't forget after I left Kentucky twelve years ago: my manners.

My mama and daddy always made sure that I used manners everywhere I went. It was something I took pride in.

"Oh, dear. Don't call me ma'am." She winked. "I'm Agnes." She tapped the nameplate before she slid the window shut. The door next to the window opened. "Betts called me this morning and told me you'd be here. But my noggin sometimes forgets little details."

She was the cutest thing. She stood only five foot tall, and she wore a simple button-down dress and thick-soled white shoes.

"I thought I'd bring donuts. I had to stop by the Cookie Crumble on my way here when I saw it was open. I was dying for a sweet treat this morning." I handed her the box.

"My grandson loves that place." She took the box and opened it, sticking her nose in it and lifting her chin back up with a grin on her face. "Cinnamon and sugar. My favorite."

"Why don't you take one for your grandson before you put them out?" I pointed back to the van outside. "I've got to get the supplies."

"Mmmhhhh." She gestured with her finger for me to go on and licked her lips, not taking her eyes off the box of sweet treats.

I popped open the back door of the van and read the note Betts had left. Betts wrote that Agnes had all the inside scoop on anything and everything, including what needed to be cleaned.

When I walked back in, there was already a slew of police officers gathered around the table. They didn't even bother looking my way.

"Already a hit and not even cleaned a thing." Agnes winked from her perch at the window.

I went about the business of looking busy, but I was really looking around to see where the prisoners were kept.

"What are you looking for?" Agnes had walked over to me. "I can help. Betts had mentioned that she didn't think you'd been in here before and to help if you needed it."

"I was wondering where the prisoners were, that's all." I smiled, trying to throw Agnes off.

"You mean you want to talk to Tammy Jo Bentley because that's the only person in our cell. If you call it a cell." There was a twinkle in her eyes.

"Am I that obvious?" I asked.

"I recognized your name when Betts told me you'd be here. I file all the notes from the detective reports." She tapped her temple. "Like I said, my noggin ain't that great, but if I remember correctly, you, Mae West, are the one who found Camille Braun."

"Unfortunately. But the problem is that I'm not even friends with Tammy Jo. I went to her house to clean for Betts like I'm doing here, and now I have to take care of her dog. I wanted to ask her some questions about Fifi's care. I mean, she's this fancy poodle." I took my phone out of my pocket and swiped to the photos. "Look here. I had to take a picture. I have to put feminine pads on the dog during her menstrual cycle."

Agnes had a pair of glasses dangling from a chain around her neck. She pulled them on her nose and looked at my photo.

"I've seen a lot in my days working here, but that's crazy." She leaned in a little closer.

"I just have a couple of questions. Do you think I could talk to her?" I asked with dipped eyebrows.

"You better hurry up. Those donuts are good, but they won't hold them off forever." Her chin slid past her shoulder, and she looked at the group of men sipping their coffee and stuffing their faces with the cinnamon and sugar treats. "Right on through that door."

"I don't need a key?" I asked.

"Mae West, this is Normal, Kentucky. Not Compton." She made a funny, and I had to smile. I liked Agnes. She wasn't just cute, she was snarky. My kind of spunky older lady. "Besides, I told Hank that Tammy Jo didn't kill no one. Look at them nails of hers. Perfect to a T."

"Camille was stabbed. Tammy Jo could easily have stabbed her and not even gotten a chip." I did a stabbing motion and took notice of my fingernails.

"Tammy Jo had her and Fifi's nails done at Cute-icles about an hour before the anonymous call to dispatch. She doesn't get the quick gel slapped on either. She gets the full package, fake nails with shellac. Helen Pyle said that Tammy Jo is driven to Cute-icles and picked up. Helen also said that Tammy keeps her calendar clear after their appointment for at least two hours to let their nails dry."

She glanced over her shoulder at the officers still stuffing their faces. She put her hand on a file.

"If I can't get Hank to see that Tammy didn't do it, maybe you can." She slid the file closer to the edge of the desk. "I remember Hank talking about how the community really embraced you when you moved here. It used to get his gills that people would talk to you and not him."

She tapped the file, and I looked down at it. Camille Braun was written on it. My eyes snapped up, my mouth open in surprise. I'd never considered I'd get to look at the file.

"I'm going to the bathroom. You can go on and clean." She gave a sweet smile and excused herself from any sort of snooping I was about to do because she couldn't lie if someone did catch me.

There was obviously something she wanted me to see if she was going to great lengths to get me to look at the file.

I plopped the bucket of cleaning supplies up on her desk, and when I felt like no one was paying attention to me, I put the file deep inside. With the broom and bucket in my grip, I headed toward the room where Tammy Jo was being held.

Instead of going right on in, I ducked into a corner and opened the file. The coroner's report said that Camille Braun had only been dead for about half an hour. That might not seem like a big deal and wouldn't get Tammy Jo off the suspect list. But as a woman who took getting her nails done very seriously, this told me and Agnes there was no way Tammy Jo did it because it didn't give her enough time for her nails to dry.

"Did you find the sink okay?" Agnes peeked her gray head around the corner and jutted it out a couple of times like a cuckoo clock. Her eyes drew down to the file. "Let me take you to her."

"I read the coroner's report." I could feel the tension rising up within me. "You and me, we know how important our nails are. But why didn't Tammy Jo tell him that?" I asked.

We passed the interrogation room on our way into a room with one cell. Tammy Jo was sitting on the bed with her legs crossed.

"I'll be back in a few minutes. That's all the time you have," Agnes warned. "Hank will be in soon, and you've not even emptied the trash. That'll be the only thing they notice in case you don't get to the rest."

Was Agnes giving me a pass on cleaning?

"Mae, what are you doing here?" Tammy Jo beamed at me. "Is something wrong with Fifi?" She lifted the back of her hand to her forehead. "Don't tell me." She threw herself back on the cot. "I can't take it."

"No. She's fine. See." I took my phone out and showed her the pictures I'd taken of Fifi.

Tammy Jo pushed herself back up and walked over to the cell bars. I held the phone between the bars and let her take a look.

"She's so cute. She really enjoys playing with the little kids in the campground." I couldn't help but smile at the memory.

"She's a dirty mess." She gave me a disapproving look. The line between her brows creased. "I'm sorry. Thank you for taking care of her."

"She misses you." I wasn't sure if I believed it because Fifi did look very comfortable in my camper.

Tammy Jo perked up. "Really?"

I nodded and looked at my phone. I'd already eaten up a lot of minutes talking about Fifi.

"I'm here filling in for Betts." I glanced back at the door to make sure we were still alone. "I wanted to make sure you were okay."

"I'm a little sore. I'm not used to sleeping on that. I have a feather bed at home." She tried to convince me she was okay, but the dark circles under her eyes told another story.

"I talked to Camille the day I was at your house cleaning. She told me about the fancy pocket watch and how much it was worth. I also heard that your watch was stolen. Do you think she was killed over the watch?" I asked.

"My lawyer told me not to talk to anyone." She nibbled on her lips like she was trying to keep something in, but it was bursting to get out.

"I know Ava. She did bring Fifi over. And it's no secret I helped find my ex-husband's killer. If you want to get home to your beloved Fifi, maybe I can help you get out of here quicker." I reached over and touched her fingernails. "I know that you were at Cute-icles the morning of the murder and you don't do anything for a few hours after, much less kill someone. Unless Camille had stolen the watch."

"No." She gripped the bars, not turning to face me. She shook her head. "There's no way Camille stole the watch. Even though the camera shows that she took it."

"Camera?" I asked.

"Yes. There're cameras all over my house. Hank had come over the day you were cleaning because I wanted to hire him for more security for the KKA event." Her head dropped. "I'll be kicked out of the association now."

"Not if you let me help you," I said. "Do you have a camera in the office?" I asked.

"No. I have one on the watch and outside. That's why I'm here. Hank looked at the footage and arrested me after my fight with Camille was caught on tape." She blinked several times.

"Why did you fight with her?" Some hesitancy was rising in my stomach. I didn't want to overstep in my questioning her, but I had to know.

"She took the watch out of the dome before Clark Wait, the horologist, stopped by. She knows that's a no-no." She clutched her chest. "I took it from her and put it back, but not without telling her that if she touched it again, that'd be the last thing she ever touched."

"Back up. Tell me why you have a horologist coming by?"

"Each day, Fifi's schedule is based on the tick of the watch. The dome allows the clock hands to echo a tick loud enough for just a dog to hear. Fifi is trained to the tick. I have a horologist come by every day during Fifi's naptime so she won't be disturbed. Clark winds the watch and makes sure it's in perfect working order. After all, Fifi is from a long line of good breeding."

"Did Fifi go down for a nap after you got back from Cute-icles?" I asked.

"Yes, Fifi was napping. Clark was on his way, and I'd had a visitor…" She abruptly stopped talking. Her mouth widened in a dramatic O, and her face drained of color. She pushed off the bars and eased back onto the cot.

"Are you talking about the woman visiting you before I showed up for the check?" I asked and caught the look of shock on her face.

"That woman has nothing to do with this. So, you just forget that you ever saw those wineglasses." She was smarter than I was giving her credit for. "Camille Braun knew that the watch was worth 2.2 million dollars. That watch is gone. If Hank Sharp finds the watch, he will find the killer."

"That woman had nothing to do with the KKA?" I asked.

"No." Her voice was tight as she spoke.

"What about the scratches on your arm? Just admit it if you struggled with Camille." I had to know everything if I was truly going to try to help her.

She stood there for a second as though she were trying to remember what I was talking about. Her jaw dropped, and her eyes popped wide open.

"Fifi just had her nails done. Just like your nails, they need to be filed. Fifi's nails were clipped, but her nails are filed by walking on the concrete. I don't let Cute-icles file them because a natural file brings her nails to perfection, making her worth more and more." She looked down at her arm and rotated it toward me. "See. There's a couple lines from the edges of her nails."

There were two rows of small scabs on her forearm exactly where I'd seen Fifi resting when I'd first shown up to clean for Betts.

"Did you even know anything about the watch on the mantel?" she asked with a curious look in her eyes.

"No clue. I know one thing for sure. If it were my watch, I'd have it in a locked drawer. Not out in the open." I took a few steps back and looked out the window of the door. I had to be extra careful not to get caught.

"Your average person has no idea. They think it's some silly little watch that my husband had." She let out a heavy sigh. "I've said too much."

"Is it true that you're leaving the watch for Fifi if you die?" I asked.

"It is. Dog breeding isn't cheap. There's good stock out there, and I've got to get Fifi the best male to sire her children. This money will help her leave a true champion legacy." She talked as if Fifi were a royal princess or queen.

"You don't have any family who know Fifi is getting your money and might want to seek revenge?" I was grasping at anything to look into.

"No one but my employees knew." She tapped a finger per name. "Ralphie, Camille, and Norman. Now, you and Ava Cox."

Ralphie, the gardener. I jerked my head when I heard Hank's voice.

"The day I came to clean, I overheard Camille and Ralphie. Did you know they were an item?" I asked.

"Of course, I did," she said. "They think they're so sneaky, but when you live alone, you hear everything. I think she was dating someone else and giving him the runaround."

"She told him she couldn't see him anymore because she didn't want to risk her job or you finding out. That Fifi was everything to her." I blinked a few times while I tried to think of the exact words but put that aside because I knew I had to hurry before Hank caught me. "He did truly threaten her."

"Ralphie?" Tammy Jo's chin ducked to the side, and she looked at me under her brows. "Trust me. I want to get out of here, but Ralphie wouldn't hurt a fly. In fact, I've tried to get him to kill ants in my garden, and he puts down this organic stuff that I swear costs me a fortune and doesn't work."

There was some rumbling around outside in the hall.

"I've got to go but know that Fifi is in great hands. I promise to take good care of her until you get out of here." I rushed out of the room and quickly picked up the duster from the bucket. I'd left it in the corner where Agnes had found me reading the file.

I pressed my lips together as an onslaught of emotions swirled inside me. I knew Tammy Jo was innocent. Camille was dead. The gardener and Camille had a very serious conversation while I was at the house, cleaning. Then there was Norman. He was the insurance man. What could he possibly know? A shiver ran through me like I could tell I was onto something, but what?

I turned around in time to see Norman, accompanied by Hank Sharp, being led into the room where Tammy Jo was being held. Frustration came off Norman in waves. I busied myself with the duster, going along the baseboards and heading toward the front of the department.

The whole ride back into downtown, I contemplated which employee knew what and what they had to gain from stealing the watch. If Hank hadn't found the watch, was he holding Tammy Jo on circumstantial evidence? If that was the case, she'd be out in less than twenty-four hours, and Fifi would be a fluffball of my past. Norman was her insurance man. He'd for sure have to answer some questions that could prove vital.

That's when I decided it was time to pay him a visit. And I knew exactly where his office was. Next to the Laundry Club. I took advantage of the parking spot between the two shops and waited until I saw Norman walk into his office after he'd gotten back from seeing Tammy Jo.

CHAPTER TWELVE

"Can I help you?" the woman behind the half-moon counter asked when I walked into the insurance agency. Her long dark hair was caught in a low ponytail and pulled around her shoulder in a chic way. She had beautiful milk chocolate skin with big brown eyes. "Do you have an appointment?"

"No." I looked around. Norman did well for himself, I thought, noticing all the rich textured furniture in the front office space. "I was hoping to talk to Norman."

There were a few couches with fabric matching the curtains in the front window of the old home. The white trim popped against the deep gray walls.

"I'm sorry. You need an appointment. Mr. Pettleman is a busy man." Her fingers clicked along the keyboard of her computer. "I can get you in next week. What type of insurance were you wanting to talk about?"

"Fifi Bentley's insurance." When she jerked her eyes away from the computer monitor, I knew I had her attention. "I'm currently taking care of Fifi Bentley while Tammy Jo is unable to. I live in a campground, and Fifi really loves to run around, and I want to make sure my allowing her to do so is okay." I pulled my phone out and pulled up the photo of Fifi. The one with the diaper and the dirty paws. "Look how cute she is with those dirty paws. She *loves* the mud."

"Let me see if Mr. Pettleman can fit you in real fast." She picked up the phone, turned her head away from me, curling her palm around the receiver, and whispered. She turned around and gently placed the phone back in the holder. "Mr. Pettleman will be right out."

"Thank you," I chirped and put the phone into my back pocket.

There wasn't even enough time for me to walk around and see what all the framed newspaper articles were about before Norman appeared.

"Ms. West." Norman headed straight toward me with his arm outstretched, his eyes staring into mine. "Is something wrong with Fifi?"

"Can we talk in your office?" I asked when I felt the receptionist trying to listen. Though her head was down, her eyes were piercing from under her brows.

"Absolutely." He lowered his hand toward my back and the other toward the hall he came from. He looked at the receptionist.

"The first conference room on the right is open." She nodded with a smile.

"Thank you, Debra," he said and gently touched my back. "This way." He offered a smile.

"Thanks for fitting me in. Debra said you were booked." I walked beside him down the hall and entered the room on the right. I took a seat in the first leather chair along the long conference table. Norman sat down across from me.

"Can I get you something to drink?" he asked.

"No, thank you. I've got to get back to the campground. Today is the Summer Sizzler party. You should stop by," I suggested.

"Thank you, but I am swamped." He folded his hands together and set them on top of the table. "Is something wrong with Fifi?" he asked again.

"Actually, no. She's having a good time. Getting in a lot of playtime and dirty paws." I thought he'd love to hear that she was happy.

"That's not good. She is a show dog from a line of elite breeding. She needs to be on her strict schedule. I told Tammy Jo this wasn't a good idea when she insisted you take her." There was an edge of anger in his tone. The muscles spasmed furiously in his jaw. "Do you understand what I'm saying?"

"She's fine. I'm actually not here to talk about her. I'm here to ask you about the watch." I watched him ease back in the chair, unfolding his hands and placing each one on the arms of the chair. "The 2.2-million-dollar watch."

"I'm aware of the watch you're talking about. Unfortunately, the watch has been stolen, and Detective Sharp is working on that. Unless," he said, sitting up again, "you know where it is."

"I have no idea. I'm trying to help Ava Cox and Tammy Jo with her case." I was lying through my teeth, though I did risk Norman going to ask her about it. "Tammy Jo said that she caught Camille stealing it. Do you really think she was stealing it?"

"I have no idea what the dog nanny was doing with it. All I know is the day you stopped by to clean, she called me and Detective Sharp to come over. She was frantic. She said to us that she'd caught Camille with the watch, and since she was hosting the KKA, she wanted extra security." So that was why she wanted security.

"I'm assuming you have the insurance policy for the watch." I leaned forward, propping my elbows up on the table.

"Yes. I hold all of Tammy Jo's policies." He nodded.

"What policies does she have?" I asked. His eyes narrowed. "I'm trying to figure out what she had in case someone is blackmailing her or had Camille working for them. See," I said, scooting to the edge of the chair, "I went back the morning of the murder to get the money Tammy Jo owed me for cleaning. When I got there, the front door was cracked open, and I found Tammy Jo on the back porch."

"Okay." He hesitated. "That's not unusual for her to be on the back porch."

"It wasn't that. It was the two wineglasses and plate of cheese that caught my eye. I know one of the glasses belonged to Tammy Jo because of the specific color of lipstick." I didn't go into detail about how, in my previous life, I'd spent a lot of money on different lipsticks and knew my colors. "The other wineglass had a bright orange lipstick stain. When I asked Tammy Jo about it, she was a little fidgety. I think she's hiding something. Protecting someone."

"Really?" He sat back up. "You asked her about it?"

"Yes." Dang. I shouldn't have said that because I didn't technically have clearance to talk to her. "I was cleaning the police station today, and I took some time to visit with her. She looks good." Lied again. "She saw the photos of Fifi, and she was happy to see her. Do you think someone for the KKA knew the watch was what kept Fifi on her schedule and stole it because they have a dog they want to take the top breeding spot?"

This was a conspiracy theory I'd just pulled out of my you-know-what, but it sounded pretty valid.

"Interesting." He stared off over my shoulder as though he were pondering my theory. "You're saying they don't care about the price tag."

"Right? I mean, it's insured, so no real loss on Tammy Jo's part." Suddenly, I felt a little over my head and wondered if I should just go back to see Hank at the department to let him know my thoughts. "She'll get some of the money back, right?"

He nodded.

"Can I see the policy? I'd like to get a watch to help with Fifi. You know, being off her schedule and all might hurt her if we wait too long." I did want to get my hands on the policy and see exactly how much it was insured for.

My stomach took a quick turn, and it soured when I remembered what Camille had told me about Tammy Jo mortgaging her house so she could get Fifi cloned for the breeding DNA.

It was the first time I wondered if Tammy Jo had done something with the watch. Was she seeing the writing on the wall that Fifi wasn't going to have a litter? Got desperate and did something with the watch? Did Camille know?

"I'm sorry. I can't let you see anything without my client's permission." He pushed himself up to stand. "I'm sure if Detective Hank wants to see them, he'll get the proper paperwork from my client." He walked over to the door.

It was an obvious cue that my time with him was over.

"Thank you for your time. I'll try to keep Fifi from the lake. She is itching to jump in." I smiled, hiding the frustration that was bubbling up inside of me.

There was something Norman and Tammy Jo were hiding. When I needed some answers, I knew the gals at the Laundry Club would at least send me in the right direction. Since it was next door to Norman's insurance agency, it was the perfect time to stop by.

I swung open the door to the laundromat and let the cool breeze of the air conditioner flood over me.

"I predict a big bowl of water with suds bubbling over is in your future." Queenie French sat at the card table to the right of the front door of the Laundry Club. Her hand was waving over the fake glass globe. Her red headband was losing its grip, her hair falling into her eyes. "I heard about Fifi Bentley staying with you." She raised a brow.

"Gosh." I sat down in the seat next to her, letting out an exhausted sigh. "I can't believe that Tammy Jo thinks I can care for that dog. Do you know that she's mortgaged her house to have the dog's DNA cloned?"

It was something I couldn't wrap my head around.

"Oh, dear." Queenie pushed the headband back in place. "I'd heard she'd gone crazy since Harrison had divorced her."

"Divorced her? Wha… whaa…" I'd suddenly became tongue-tied.

Queenie's chin tilted down to her chest, the lines in her forehead creased, and her eyes widened. It appeared she was trying to figure out what I was saying.

I gulped and heaved in a big breath of air. My brain needed oxygen. Was Harrison involved in this? I couldn't make a complete thought.

"He's dead now." Queenie shrugged.

"Oh my God, Queenie." I put my hand up to my chest. "You nearly gave me a heart attack. I'd already figured him alive and thought he was the one who stole his own watch."

"Stole a watch?" She was all sorts of confused. "Does this call for a pot of coffee?" She jumped up. There wasn't a better time for a cup of coffee. Even in the Indian summer heat.

Queenie busied herself with the coffeepot and talked to the customers near the coffee station. I overheard her telling them to change the television channel or help themselves to the coffee, puzzles, and books.

"Make yourself at home." Her voice echoed across the laundromat.

I was trying to figure out why Tammy Jo had told me the office was that of her deceased husband. I guess, he was dead, but she clearly left out the part about the divorce. That made my suspect list even bigger. Did he remarry? Did he have children? If so, did they think they should get the pocket watch? It was, after all, 2.2 million dollars. And if that wasn't enough to kill for, I wasn't sure what was.

There was no time to have coffee. I was already late for the Summer Sizzler party, and Dottie would be mad, but I knew how to soften her up: gossip. If anyone in Normal knew anything about Tammy Jo and Harrison Bentley's divorce, it'd be her. She was like the CEO of gossip around here.

"Queenie," I called over to her. "I've completely lost track of time. Dottie will kill me if I miss any more of the party." I waved when she shooed me out the door.

CHAPTER THIRTEEN

Happy Trials Campground had cars lined up from the entrance to the office. The sounds of a bluegrass band echoed off the mountains in the Daniel Boone National Forest. When I got closer, I pulled the Ford up to the office. There were so many people walking around the campground that I didn't want to drive the car all the way to my camper while dodging guests.

Ken and Magdalene Heidelman were standing near the storage units. I headed over there to welcome them back and make sure he'd gotten the paperwork for the new insurance policy to add a pool to the campground. I knew it would cost a lot of money, but I felt like it would add a great deal of value to Happy Trails.

"Are you here for a while?" I asked when I walked up to them.

"We are going to be here for a couple of weeks." Magdalene tugged at the ends of her short blond hair. She was in her midsixties. The other hand gripped the handle of a bucket with some cleaning supplies in it. "I told Ken that he needed to get out of that office."

"I'm fine, but now that we are here, I'm glad she insisted." He winked and rubbed his hand down his wife's back. They were such a sweet couple.

"We're getting our golf cart out." She handed him a set of keys to unlock the storage unit.

"If you need anything, please let me know." I watched Ken lift the door. He and Magdalene worked like a well-oiled machine. He had his duties and she had hers.

Before she let him start the golf cart, she used a few wipes to clean off the seat and sprayed some glass cleaner on the windshield.

"Did you get the pool paperwork I faxed you?" I asked Ken after he'd pulled the cart out of the storage unit. Magdalene busied herself with locking up the unit.

"Pool?" Norman Pettleman came around the corner. Ken and I both looked at him. "Mae. Ken." He shook Ken's hand. "You're putting in a pool? That's costly."

"I think it'll add a nice touch to the campground. If my client wants a pool, it's my job to help get it insured." Ken looked at me and smiled. "It'll be fine."

"I'm sure it will." Norman turned to me. "I'm here to check on Fifi before I go see Tammy Jo."

"She's been great." I wasn't about to tell him that I didn't feed her the yucky food that was in her bag. "Would you like to see her?"

"That'd be great." He clasped his hands behind his back and swiveled his body toward Ken. "It was good seeing you, Ken. Let's grab a beer while you're in town."

"Sounds good. I'd like to get your take on the new insurance plan for the condos they've put in place." The two talked shop. When I realized they were going to be a minute, I excused myself, but not without telling Norman that I'd be right back.

There were still cars entering the campground for the Summer Sizzler party, and it tickled me to death that these monthly gatherings were becoming more and more popular.

"Where have you been?" Dottie Swaggert ran out of the office. She put her hands on her hips, shifting her weight from side to side with a big scowl on her face. "Bobby Ray has plugged up his toilet, and I'm not fixing it. Henry is too busy doing what I need him to do today while this Summer Sizzler is going on."

"I had to clean the police station for Betts this morning. I'll go take a look at it." When I heard the sound of a woman singing, I put my hand to my eyes to shield them from the sun so I could get a better look at the band. "Blue Ethel and the Adolescent Farm Boys?" I looked at Ethel.

"She might look old and have tinted blue hair, but she's good and cheap." Her tensed jaw melted. "Everyone is having a good time. All the campers have different foods to offer. Ty has the hog going near the dock. Before I forget, I gave Ty the extra set of keys to your camper so the boys could play with Fifi."

She pointed to the lake where Fifi was running between the two boys as they threw the beach ball to each other. She was yipping and jumping in delight. This was probably the best time the poor girl had ever had.

"Speaking of Fifi. I wanted to ask you about Tammy Jo Bentley and her deceased husband. I mean, I thought she was married to him when he died, but apparently, she wasn't."

I thought for sure I'd opened the floodgate for Dottie to yammer on and on about it, but she sat there, stone-faced, looking at me. The office door opened, and a beautiful blond woman walked out. Her blond hair was straight and polished. Definitely not from a bottle. She had salon and spa written all over her Tory Burch orange outfit and double-T orange sandals to match, leaving my stomach in a jealous twinge.

"Dottie, the phone was ringing, and I answered it. I took a message for a reservation and left it on your desk." Her crystal-blue eyes looked at me, and she smiled. The orange on her lips perfectly matched her outfit. Yeah. She had money. "Hi, you must be Mae West." She stuck her hand out. "I'm Nicki Swaggert."

"Nicki Swagg…" There I went again. Tongue-tied. I should've recognized those eyes from Ty's yearbook. I gulped. "Ty's Nicki Swaggert?" I couldn't stop my mind from releasing the words from my mouth, and I suddenly felt dizzy.

"Oh, Ty." She even had a cute laugh that made me feel ridiculous and sick. "That was so long ago, but I do have to say that I'm looking forward to catching up with him over a drink."

"A drink?" My mouth dried. My vision narrowed, and I felt my hands fist at my side. "So you don't live in Normal?"

"No. I live in Atlanta. I'm a doctor."

Of course you are, I thought, as I imagined running her over with my camper. It wasn't nice. I knew that, but I couldn't help it.

"I'm only here to visit since my mother is in trouble."

"Your mother?" I looked at Dottie. "Are you in trouble?"

"Oh, gosh." Nicki put her delicate and lovely hand on Dottie's arm. "She's like a mother to me, but Dottie is my stepmother. She made my father so happy."

"Who is your mother?" I blinked rapidly, suddenly needing to know everything about Nicki, including this drink date with Ty.

"Tammy Jo Bentley is my mother, and I understand that she trusted you with my precious little sister." She winked and smiled. Her teeth twinkled; they were such a bright white.

"You!" I gasped. "Orange lipstick and wineglass."

How on earth had I not put the two together when she walked out of the office a while ago.

"I think the sun is getting to Mae." Dottie grabbed me by the elbow and walked me toward

the office. "You need air conditioning."

"Wait." I stopped moving. "You went to visit your mom the day Camille Braun was found murdered."

"Yes. I was actually just driving through town, and now that Camille has turned up dead, I guess I need to stay here and see what's going to happen with Mother." Nicki's lashes fluttered. I leaned in a little closer to see if those were fake. Nope. No chance. My stomach twinged again.

"Can I see you in the office for a second? Alone." I looked at Dottie and didn't wait for her to answer me.

"Are you okay?" Dottie shut the door behind her.

"No. I. Am. Not." I jutted my pointer finger toward the door. "You didn't tell me that you were married to Tammy Jo's ex-husband and that Nicki Swaggert was your stepdaughter."

"You never asked," she said in a calm voice. "Harrison and I aren't proud that we fell in love at the end of his marriage."

"But when I moved here, you told me you didn't have any money and all the money you had was stolen from my ex-husband." I reminded her about how I gave her money.

"Tammy Jo had her own money. The only thing Harrison had was that stupid pocket watch that he let Tammy Jo train the dog with. He agreed to let her will it to the dog, never figuring he was going to die first. There wasn't a stipulation in the will about the watch upon his death. Since he let Tammy Jo have everything in their divorce, she gets the watch after Fifi dies." Dottie sucked in a deep breath. "Fifi is going to outlive all of us." She turned her head to look out the window toward the lake. "Oh, no!"

I looked out the window. Timmy Randal had Fifi on her leash. He was bent over laughing at the brown-and-white pug and Fifi playing. On closer inspection, they weren't playing. They were doing something that God never intended for a pug and a poodle to do.

"No!" I bolted out the door of the office and ran as fast as I could toward Timmy. "Stop!" I screamed and flailed my arms over my head like a madwoman. Somewhere along the way, I lost my hair band, and my long curly hair sprang out from my head. I could only imagine what I looked like because Blue Ethel and the Adolescent Farm Boys stopped playing, and everyone turned around to look at me.

"They were just playing," Timmy said and started to cry. The two dogs pulled away, and Fifi growled at the pug.

"Who does this dog belong to?" I asked with a stiff upper lip, trying not to cry.

"Rosco is our dog." Ethel of Blue Ethel and the Adolescent Farm Boys had come off the stage. "What happened?"

"Are you Ethel of the Smelly Dog?" I pinched my eyes shut in hopes she wasn't but, it was becoming very clear almost everyone I knew in Normal had more than one job. Ethel Biddle was probably no different.

"I sure am. Do you have a dog?" She reached down and patted Rosco. He snorted, grunted, and then farted. Just like a man after doing what he'd just done.

"No. You've done enough damage," I groaned.

Poor Fifi. I grabbed her leash away from Timmy. He ran off hysterically crying toward Ty, who was now making his way over to us.

I grabbed Fifi and darted off to the camper, but not without noticing Norman Pettleman shaking his head in disapproval. The entire way over, I prayed and prayed really hard. *Please, God. I'm begging. Please don't let Fifi be pregnant with Rosco's babies. Tammy Jo will kill me if Fifi's designer breeding has been ruined and she loses her house for good.*

"Mae!" Ty jogged up beside me. "What on earth happened?"

"I don't want to speak it into existence." I jerked Fifi closer to me. "Besides, shouldn't you be getting ready for your drink with Nicki, or are you going to go after we have supper? Or are you going to break that off with me?"

"Stop right there." He jumped in between me and the camper door. "I don't know what's going on here. I feel like you're mad at me, and I didn't do anything. Neither did Timmy." He pointed to the picnic table that was under my camper awning. "Please, just sit down for a minute and talk to me. Then I'll let you do whatever you need to do."

Fifi squirmed in my arms until I finally let her down. She darted out from underneath the awning when I sat down on the bench, but the leash brought her back when it was stretched to its maximum length. Ty didn't take his eyes off of me. He sat down next to me. I dizzied from his smell, and my heart softened.

"I'm sorry. I shouldn't have yelled at Timmy, but Rosco had taken advantage of Fifi." I looked up at him and made my eyes big to emphasize what I meant.

"Advantage of? As in sex?" As he questioned me, his chin got lower and lower.

"Exactly. Poor girl." I bit back tears.

Ty Randal apparently thought it was the funniest thing he'd ever heard because he was literally bent over from laughing so hard.

"I'm glad you find this so funny," I said, trying to keep a straight face, but his laughter was so infectious that I, too, started to laugh. "It sounds so ridiculous," I admitted. The tears falling down my face were from laughing.

It took a few minutes until we'd gotten ourselves together. Rosco had sniffed his way over to the camper.

"No. No," I warned the dog. "You've done enough damage."

"Aw, he's smitten with her." Ty smiled at the dogs. "The damage is already done."

"How on earth am I going to explain this to Tammy Jo? She'll have to go on suicide watch," I said, half joking, half not. "Her beloved, DNA-insured Fifi will not be continuing the prized line of breeding."

"Insured?" He started to laugh again. "That's even funnier."

"No. It's really not." I gnawed my lip and looked at the two dogs. Fifi was prancing around on the tips of her fancy painted toes like she knew she was messing with a dog from the seedy side of town and that her mother was never going to approve of it.

"I think Camille Braun was killed over this pocket watch that Fifi is trained by," I continued, watching his face go into some different contorted positions. He clearly couldn't believe what I was telling him. "It was Harrison Swaggert's, and I had no idea he was Dottie's deceased husband or that Nicki was her stepdaughter."

I had to reel in my frustration. None of this was Ty's fault. Not yet anyway.

"The watch is missing. It's been stolen. It's worth 2.2 million dollars. The watch goes to Fifi per the divorce papers. Fifi comes from a line of top poodle breeding, and Tammy Jo has mortgaged her house as leverage to have Fifi's DNA cloned." My jaw dropped. "Maybe she's already had her cloned, and we can just use that instead of her offspring." I jerked the leash when I noticed Rosco sniffing in places he didn't need to sniff.

The fat dog with the smushed face waddled off, farting the entire way. I looked over the party. Ethel was back to belting out tunes. Bobby Ray was doing some sort of jig in front of the stage. Smacking his leg, jerking up one foot at a time in beat with the band. People were eating, laughing, and really having a good time. I would've too if it weren't for an angelic Nicki Swaggert swaying to the music with her face up to the sun, looking like a goddess.

I looked back at Ty. He too was focused on Nicki.

"Listen, I can't go tonight. I'm sorry, but I've got to go look at one of the toilets in one of the bungalows." I left out that it was Bobby Ray's clogged toilet. "I really need to be here for Fifi too."

"Alright. I'm not going to beg you to let me take you for supper just so I can apologize for leaving last time." He made it very clear we weren't going on a date, something I blamed on Nicki Swaggert. "Let me know if you change your mind." When he stood up and ran his hand through his hair, his bicep popped. My heart fell into my stomach.

"I won't." One thing about me, when I made my mind up, I made my mind up. Nicki made it no secret that she and Ty were going to enjoy a drink. Who was I to stop the high school reunion?

I watched Ty walk off. He was almost to the lake when I saw his hand fly up. Nicki was across the other side near the band, waving him over. He didn't hesitate one bit. He took her cue and headed right toward her.

Watching her grab his hand and him twirling her around in circles made me sick. Sick enough to get ready to plunge Bobby Ray's crap.

CHAPTER FOURTEEN

I f I'd known running a campground was like running a daycare, I might've just sold the darn thing when I had the chance. Especially now that I stared down at the great unknown in the porcelain throne in Bobby Ray's bungalow.

Me and the plunger were in for the fight of our lives. I put all I had into pushing the tool up and down as the brown, murky water gurgled and splashed. A few times I gagged and had to look back at Fifi. I didn't dare leave her in the camper or, even worse, let Timmy Randal watch her again. We all saw how that turned out.

Fifi wasn't impressed. She tap-danced on the floor and decided to test the length of the leash that I'd tied to the bathroom door handle.

"If it weren't for your rebellious ways, you could still be out there enjoying the fun." I waved the plunger around, gagging at the drips coming off of it.

Fifi looked back at me, and I swear she was judging me with her high-dollar eyes. She turned and started to sniff around the floor.

"I'm glad Ethel buzzed off the ball on your tail." I know she didn't understand me, but it made me feel better.

I went back to take a few more jabs to clear the clog. I rocked back and forth on my heels as the plunger sucked and released, finding a groove. There were some things that came out of my mouth that probably shouldn't, at least not in front of Betts Hager and the Bible Thumpers.

"Seriously. I wonder if that buyer still wants a campground," I grunted just as something flew out of the toilet, hit my shirt, and then landed on the ground.

Fifi scurried back into the bathroom and snatched up whatever it was.

"Gross!" I yelled and said a few more swear words. Not only had Fifi gotten dirty, she was probably knocked up by Tammy Jo's enemy's pug and was now eating whatever it was that came out of Bobby Ray.

She looked up at me. There was something dangling from her mouth.

"Drop it," I insisted and snapped my finger at her. Just like that, she opened her tiny little mouth, dropping a pocket watch on the bathroom floor. I looked back and forth from the toilet to the pocket watch that looked awfully similar to the one stolen from Tammy Jo's.

All sorts of *ews* and more *ewwws* came out of me when I took a piece of toilet paper and picked up the pocket watch, dangling it in the air to get a better look. There was no way I was going to run water over it or even try to see if it worked for fear I'd damage it even more.

I quickly untied the leash from the doorknob with one hand. Bobby Ray's toilet was going to have to wait. He had a lot of explaining to do about why this pocket watch was down his toilet.

I was temporarily blinded when I stepped out of the bungalow. I blinked a few times to get rid of the big black dots and tried to get some fresh air into my lungs. I caught sight of myself in the glass of the bungalow's door. While my bushy hair and the wet spot on my shirt hadn't done it, hearing Nicki Swaggert's laughter as she swung her hair back and forth in front of Hank Sharp sent me into a spiral.

I bolted across the campground with my arm extended in front of me, the toilet paper flying around my hand, the watch dangling, Fifi's little legs trying to keep up with me, and my medusa hair bouncing around. It was a pretty picture for sure. I'd really seen better days.

"Where did you get that?" Bobby Ray stopped me before I even got to the boat dock.

Over his shoulder, I could see Hank turn. His eyes focused on me. He said something to Nicki and started to make his way toward us. He took his phone from his pocket and made a call.

"Where did you get this?" I shoved the watch in front of Bobby Ray's face.

"It was a gift." He shrugged.

"From who?" I asked, a little more irritated.

"It doesn't matter." His jaw tensed. His eyes darkened.

"You shoved a gift down my toilet and clogged it. I've got God knows what all over my shirt, and this watch that looks eerily similar to the 2.2-million-dollar watch that was stolen from Tammy Jo Bentley's house exploded out of my bungalow's toilet. So, yes, it does matter who gave it to you."

"Excuse me." Hank Sharp's green eyes hardened. "Bobby Ray Bond?"

"Who wants to know?" Bobby Ray's chest puffed out like a bandy rooster about to have a cock fight.

"Detective Hank Sharp." Hank grabbed Bobby by the wrist, and before he could even get out the rest of his words, he had Bobby pinned on the ground. "You are under arrest for robbery. You stay right here and play nice so I don't have to hurt you. I've already called for backup."

"I didn't rob no one." Bobby tried to jerk free with his face in the grass. "Let me go. Police bru-tality!" Bobby's voice echoed, once again, stopping Blue Ethel and the Adolescent Farm Boys's rendition of Will Smith's *Summertime*, which didn't sound good anyway. "Help me! Po-leeece bru-tality!"

"Bobby Ray, stop it," I warned. "Seriously, Hank. Let him up. He's not going anywhere."

"Yeah, dude. I'm not going anywhere. Listen to May-bell-ine." Bobby finally stopped squirming. "I'll answer any questions you need me to."

"May-bell-ine?" Hank looked at me as if that was what was impor-tant this very minute. I glared at him. He smiled, though he still had a death grip on Bobby Ray. "You swear you ain't gonna run? I've got a gun in my sock, and I'm not afraid to shoot you."

"No. May-bell-ine Grant, tell him who I am," Bobby Ray insisted.

"Bobby Ray is one of my foster brothers. He is the one who gave me the money to move to New York City when I turned eighteen. He showed up here a couple of days ago and has been living here since."

Hank seemed to ease up on his grip, but not much. His eyes focused on the dangling pocket watch.

"His bungalow toilet was clogged. I've been in there plunging it, and this came out. I recognized it from cleaning Tammy Jo's house. I was in the process of asking him how he got it when you came over here and went all ninja on him."

The sound of sirens got closer, and in the distance, I could see plumes of gravel dust rising in the air before I saw the black sedan barreling up the campground road, red light flashing in the front windshield.

Now the entire party had gathered around us and the bungalows. Dottie shook her head in disapproval as if she were reminding me that she told me Bobby Ray was bad news.

Hank didn't let him go until Detective Elmo Burke got out of the car with handcuffs they could slap on Bobby's wrists.

"Come see me in the pokey, May-bell-ine! You owe me!" Bobby hollered the entire way to the black car before Elmo shoved him in the backseat.

"Yep." Dottie saddled up to me.

"I know," I said sarcastically. "You told me."

"Mmmhhhmmm." She nodded proudly as both of us watched the taillights of the car disappear.

"You didn't tell me that Nicki, Ty's ex, was your stepdaughter." I couldn't help but glance over at Nicki, the good-time girl. I grinned when that title popped into my head. She now had the audience of Henry and Ty.

"You never asked." Dottie's brows rose.

"You love to talk about everybody else, but I notice that you've never told me anything about you." My temples began to throb. Rosco was waddling back over to us. "I've got to get Fifi in the house."

"What do you want to know, Mae?" Dottie walked beside me. "There's nothing to know. I married her father when she was out of high school and off on her own life. I only heard rumblings about her little romance with Ty, but they were kids. It was when she got back from college that she strung along both boys."

"Hank and Ty?" I gave her a sharp look.

"No different than what you've been doing." Her right eyebrow rose.

Touché. Well played, Dottie Swaggert.

I walked up the camper steps and slammed the door behind me. I got Fifi a drink of water and filled her bowl with leftovers from the refrigerator. There was no sense in giving her the good kibble Tammy Jo insisted on. She was already wearing a scarlet letter. I quickly made a pot of coffee and took the notebook where I'd been writing down my sleuthing ideas to help Tammy Jo. Apparently, it was Bobby Ray all along.

There was a knock at my door.

"I don't have anything." I stopped talking when I saw it was Hank Sharp standing at the door.

"We need to talk." He pushed his way into the camper.

"Well, come on in. Oh." I lifted my hands. "You already came in."

"Coffee, please." He sat down at the table. His eyes looked at my notebook. He groaned and shoved it off to the side. "I need you to tell me everything from the beginning about this Bobby Ray, May-bell-ine." His Southern accent was deep.

I gave him a long look. It would've been longer, but the coffeepot beeped that it was finished with the brew cycle. Right now, I needed coffee to help clear my head.

I fixed a couple of mugs and set one in front of Hank. I leaned up against the kitchen sink and took a few sips.

"He showed up here a couple of days ago. He said he'd seen the article about me in the magazine and he walked here. He needed a place to stay. I owed him that. I let him shower, I gave him a bungalow to sleep in, and I gave him back the three thousand dollars he gave me when we were kids. He insisted that I didn't owe him, but he didn't try to give it back either." I took a few more sips. "I have no idea how he got the watch."

"He's got a record." Hank informed me about his petty theft charges. "He's on camera sitting in Tammy Jo's kitchen with Camille."

Swaying a bit, I leaned back even more.

"Just hours later, Camille's seen taking the watch out for a second time, after the fight with Tammy Jo." He had a good case against Bobby Ray. "When I searched Bobby Ray's bungalow, I found a phone. There's not much on there, but there is a Google search about the Daniels watch. I haven't questioned him yet, but it appears he's likely the killer."

"The Bobby Ray I knew twelve years ago was not capable of killing someone. But I don't know him as an adult." Now I wished I'd listened to Dottie. "Can I see him?" I asked in a hushed whisper.

"I'll let you have a few minutes with him later after we question him. Do you have a to-go cup? I need to finish going through the bungalow and head back to the department." He'd gone back to being the somewhat reasonable man I'd seen a few times.

"Sure." I searched the cabinet before finally finding a to-go cup in the far back. "What about Tammy Jo?"

He poured another cup of coffee in the to-go cup.

"I guess I don't have anything to keep her on. I need to get her released too." He opened the door of the camper. "When you come down to the station, I'm going to need a formal statement from you about how you found the watch."

"Okay." I shut the door after he left and looked over at Fifi.

Her white paws were brown, and she'd had a full day, but I swear there was a smile on her face.

CHAPTER FIFTEEN

Not even a little arrest could dampen the spirits of the campers and attendees of the Summer Sizzler. Maybe it had to do with some day drinking and liquid courage. After I packed up Fifi's things, we took our last walk together down to my car that I'd parked next to the office earlier.

I didn't bother Dottie, who seemed to finally be enjoying the fruits of her labor. She had her toes dangled into the lake. Ty and his boys were in one of the pedal boats in the middle of the lake. I didn't see Nicki Swaggert anywhere. The humidity probably got to her, and she melted. Just a thought.

Fifi had her head stuck out the window the entire way across town until we pulled into the police station. I parked next to the two black sedan cars that I knew belonged to Hank and Elmo. With a twinge of sadness in my heart, I picked up Fifi and got her fancy pink, monogrammed bag. She licked my face like she knew what was happening and was begging me to keep her. It made me feel better to think that.

"Fifi!" Tammy Jo came running out the door next to Agnes's window when we walked in. She went to grab the poodle but pulled back. "Oh, what the heck." She grabbed her from me. "You might be dirty, but nothing a little bath from Camille..." She paused when she realized what she'd said. "From mommy will fix you right up."

Tammy Jo's nostrils flared with a couple of quick whiffs. She lifted Fifi up in the air and twisted the dog all around. Then... as if she were some sort of Rosco magnet, hand to God, Tammy Jo lifted Fifi's butt right up to her nose. She looked at me as if her head was about to spin off her shoulders and Satan himself was going to pop right out of her body.

"What. Did. You. Do?" She cried out. "My baby!" A bloodcurdling scream started from her toes and whipped itself up into the ugliest cry I'd ever seen come out of a grown woman. I mean, I've seen hissy fits, and this was a step way above that.

Just about then, Nicki Swaggert waltzed in with her arms outstretched, giving Tammy Jo's scream a run for its money.

"Mother! I'm taking you home." The fakest sincerity dripped right on out of her, making me sick all over again but thankful for her interruption. Her manicured hands clasped to her chest as she fluttered her long lashes at me. She tossed her hair. She'd changed into a pale green suit that fit her like it was tailored. The color brought out the tan of her skin. "We will get Fifi all back to normal."

There was still fire in Tammy Jo's eyes. When Norman Pettleman came out of one of the offices, I knew he'd told her what happened between Rosco and Fifi. Eventually, I knew I was going to have to come clean, but I had to say, I was happy to see Nicki Swaggert had come to whisk her mother out of there.

"If you think you're getting another dime from me," Tammy Jo spat, words laced with fire, "You've got another thing coming."

My ears perked up. There was something really strange going on between Tammy Jo and her daughter, as well as between Dottie and Nicki.

"Oh, Mama. We need to get you home to a good shower, and I'll bathe our sweet Fifi." Nicki patted her mom's arm and guided her out the door.

The police station was buzzing with chatter.

"I told you she didn't do it." Agnes nodded with satisfaction on her face. "And I'm not so certain this guy did it either." She tapped her temple with the wrinkled pad of her finger. "He doesn't have the brains to pull this off."

"But Hank said there's some evidence on Bobby Ray's phone, and I did find the watch in his toilet." My lips pinched so they wouldn't contort at the thought of exactly how I'd gotten the watch to come out of the commode.

Hank walked around the corner, coming face-to-face with me and Agnes.

"Granny, don't be gossiping about anything with her." He put his arm around Agnes.

"You're his granny?" My jaw dropped.

"Yep. Can you believe it?" She rolled her eyes. "You better watch it. You can't tell me who I can and can't talk to around here. You're not too big for a whoopin.'"

"Come on. I'll let you talk to Bobby Ray." Hank shook his head at his granny, and I followed him back to the cell. "I know you came here and talked to Tammy Jo."

"I was cleaning," I corrected him.

He wasn't fooled. "No. You and my granny were in cahoots."

"Being in cahoots is kinda fun." I nudged him with my elbow. "You might want to try it sometime."

"Maybe I will." There was a flirtatious tone to his voice that stopped my thoughts. Was he flirting with me? He pointed to a couple of different little boxes on the wall. "Those are video cameras. We keep them on, all the time."

"Ohhhhh," I said, dragging it out. "Then if you knew I was talking to her, why didn't you stop me?"

"Mae West," he said, letting out a long sigh and turning around at the threshold of the door to the holding room. "Somehow you get people to tell you things. I haven't figured it out. I'm not sure how you got her to trust you so much that she let you take care of her prized dog."

"You're being nice to me now because you want me to talk to Bobby Ray and tell you what he says." I wasn't stupid, and Hank Sharp was being way too nice to me this time around. He wasn't spouting about how I needed to stay out of his investigation like he'd done with Paul.

Since Paul's death, I was almost embarrassed to admit that I'd been watching too many detective and mystery television shows at night.

"I'd like to know what the two of you talk about." There was a glint in his eyes. He opened the door. The sounds of Bobby Ray Bond whistling a happy tune sounded like a songbird chirping in the early morning dawn.

"May-bell-ine, I knew you'd come." He gripped the bars of the holding cell and stuck his chin and nose through them.

"If you can get him to stop that whistling, there might be a bonus tin of coffee on your camper doorstep in the morning," Hank whispered as I passed him on the way into the holding room.

"Can we please have a few minutes alone?" I ignored Hank's request and gave him a cold hard stare.

"Sure." He backed out of the room, shutting the door behind him.

"You've got to know I didn't do this." There was sharp tone in Bobby Ray's voice. Long gone was the happy whistling. "That girl gave me that watch."

"First things first." I was taken aback that he admitted he'd had possession of the watch. I'd hoped someone had planted it in his bungalow toilet. "How on earth did you get hooked up with Camille?"

He'd left out that part of his story when he showed up at the beach on the lake that morning.

"You've got to believe me when I tell you that I was just walking here, minding my own business, when she pulled her car to the side of the road. She jumped out and asked if I needed a ride. I told her where I was going, and she said that she knew the place." He gave a sturdy nod.

"You're telling me that Camille Braun was driving along the road and gave you a ride along with the watch?" I asked.

"Not exactly. She said that she needed a favor. She needed me to help pull weeds in this garden because the person that did work in the garden had a hurt back. Since I was looking for work and on my way to come see you, I figured a day's work wouldn't hurt." Bobby Ray was never one to turn down work or a good day's wage. So this didn't strike me as strange.

The only thing strange here was the fact it just so happened to be Camille with the watch, and she was dead.

"How did you get the watch?" I asked.

"I did pull the weeds and went into the big house to get me a drink. That watch was on the mantle, and Camille caught me looking at it." He shrugged. "After that I went back to the kitchen and finished getting my drink. She made me a sandwich. By that time, it was night, and she told me I could stay in the guest house on the property."

"There's a guest house?" I wondered if Hank had been there. I waved off the silly question. Of course, he had. He was the detective after all.

"Yeah. She took me there and said she'd drop me off at the campground the next morning." He rubbed his head. "I fell right to sleep. It was nice having a bed to sleep in after I'd walked all this way."

"Please, Bobby Ray, just stick with the story. Then what happened?" I asked, knowing I had to keep him on track. He was the type of person that made a story way longer than it needed to be.

"I'm getting there, May-bell-ine." His chest heaved a deep breath. "The next day she came and got me like she said. She said that she didn't have any money at the moment but gave me the pocket watch to hold for her for a few days. I asked her why. She said that she needed to keep it safe, and when she came to get it from me, she'd pay me in cash." His brows furrowed, and the lines on his forehead deepened.

"You taking the watch was the favor?" I asked, though I wanted a confirmation.

"Yep."

"Why did you flush it?" I asked.

"You know when you passed me at the recreation center when I was getting my paper?" he asked, and I nodded. "I took my time walking back to the bungalow because it was such a nice morning. When I got back, I fixed me a cup of coffee and sat down to read the paper and look through the jobs section. That darn watch and the headline that it was stolen were on the front page. It said that Camille was killed. I swear I didn't kill that woman. I was at the campground," he said, starting to plead his case.

"Why did you flush the watch?" It was typical to need to continue to keep Bobby Ray on subject.

"I don't know what on earth it was all about, but all I know is what I've told you. I didn't want to get no one in no trouble. I had to get rid of the watch. Although I read it was worth millions, I didn't care. I can't afford to get in no more trouble."

"It's not just theft. It's murder. They think you murdered Camille for the watch now that you have admitted you worked there." I stopped dead in my tracks. "You said you went into the house and looked at the watch on the mantle. Right?"

"Yep." He pushed off the bars and paced inside.

"Did you have muddy feet?" I asked.

"Probably. I was pulling weeds. I'm telling you that I didn't kill no one." He continued to talk and talk in his Bobby Ray way, as incomplete thoughts swirled in my head.

"I'll be back." I turned on the balls of my feet.

"May-bell-ine, where are you going? Don't leave me here!" I heard him yell as I walked down the hallway to find Hank Sharp.

The police station was buzzing. The chatter was about the local television news stations outside waiting for a news conference. It looked like Hank Sharp was about to make a statement because Agnes, like a true mom, was brushing off the shoulders of his suit coat. They put a smile on my face. Hank looked over at me.

"Can I see you for a second?" I asked and gestured to a corner in the room where no one was standing.

He walked over to me.

"Did I hear something about a news crew?" I asked.

"Ava Cox called the media to let them know Tammy Jo Bentley was wrongly accused. She's trying to save Tammy Jo's position in the KKA. She also let them know the watch was found with a drifter." His jaw tensed as his eyes darted around the room. "The mayor called, and she said I have to make a statement. Apparently, the thought of a random person walking around stealing and killing people is hurting the economy."

"I've not had the pleasure to meet the mayor, but I don't think you can go out there and tell the public you have the killer." It was true. I hadn't met Courtney MacKenzie, though I'd heard she was pretty by the book, and if she wanted something done, I wasn't sure Hank would go against her.

No matter what it looked like and the evidence against Bobby Ray, I knew in my gut that he didn't do it.

"Let me guess," Hank sighed, brushing his hand through his hair. "He told you he didn't do it."

In the background, someone called Hank's name because it was time.

"I know him. Besides, he was at the campground when she was killed. I saw him earlier that morning when I went to pick up Ty Randal from the airport." My jaw dropped. I even shocked myself remembering that Bobby didn't have a car, though he could've gotten a ride. Still, I knew he didn't do it.

"I know that he's got a pretty solid alibi, if he's telling the truth," Hank said through gritted teeth. "I'm going to look into what he told me, but until then he's staying in there."

I looked over when the room went silent. You know how a room gets really quiet when a person of power walks in? Well, that was what happened when a woman with shoulder-length auburn hair and a sprinkle of freckles dotting her nose walked in.

Normally, I'd say redheads couldn't wear a red pantsuit, but this one could and did it well.

"I don't have time for this right now." Hank put both hands out to me when he noticed her.

"You need to make time, or you're going to regret it." So, my words sounded like a threat, and by the look on his face, I could see he took it as that. Then the words he'd told me so many times before came out in a rush.

"It was a mistake to tell you anything about this case." He grabbed a folder off the desk next to us. Our little corner was no longer out of sight. His actions told me in no uncertain terms what he thought of my comment and my involvement in the investigation. A vein popped out in his temple that I'd never noticed. "You need to leave and go back to your campground. Do your job, and I'll do mine."

"Detective?" Mayor MacKenzie put her hands in the front pockets of her red pantsuit. "Now."

Hank gave me a final hard look before he went to join the mayor. I stayed still until the door of the department shut, leaving me and Agnes inside alone.

"That woman sends chills up my spine every time I see her." Agnes's voice cracked.

"Someone around here likes her since they voted her in." I took a deep breath to calm my nerves. "Too bad Hank won't listen to me. I'm telling you; Bobby Ray didn't kill Camille."

"Honey, I don't know anything about cases, but I do know that something stinks about all of this." She wrinkled her nose.

A text from Abby Fawn chirped on my phone. I'd completely forgotten about the Laundry Club book club meeting. She wanted to know if I was coming. I quickly texted her back that I was on my way.

CHAPTER SIXTEEN

Agnes had showed me the back door of the police station. The last thing I needed was to walk out the front door of the station in front of all of the cameras out there. They'd spent months following me around after what happened to me when Paul went to jail and then was murdered.

The news media was so focused on Hank Sharp at the podium, they didn't even notice my little Ford drive behind them. Hank did. His eyes caught mine, and he briefly stopped talking into the microphone before taking a big gulp and continuing.

I hated to do it, but I did. I made a call to Ava Cox on my way over to the book club meeting.

"Hello, Mae," Ava greeted me with a monotone voice. "The way I figure it, we are done with our little business now that my client has been taken off the suspect list. I would like to thank you on behalf..."

"Drop it. I'm not calling about Fifi or any thank-yous. I'm calling because I need you to go get my friend Bobby Ray Bond out of jail." I heard a pause then a deep inhale on her end. Before I let her protest, because I could tell she was revving up to that, I continued, "You and I both know that you owe me since I took in Fifi when I really didn't have to."

My words were met with a bit of awkward silence. It seemed we were both waiting for the other to cave.

"How am I going to get him out when he was caught with the watch?" At least she didn't say no or hang up.

"He has an alibi. He's a longtime friend of mine, and he's staying at Happy Trails. He doesn't have a car, and before I left the campground the morning of Camille's death, he was with Henry, my maintenance man. They've barely been apart since Bobby Ray came to town." I knew it was a long shot for her to take it, so I continued to ramble on about what Bobby had told me. "I think that Camille was in some trouble."

I also told her about the conversation I'd heard between Camille and the gardener.

"I think she and the gardener had some sort of plan to take the watch and run. When Bobby Ray saw it on the mantle, I think it gave her the idea to plant it on him and say it was stolen by this random guy she hired to do some yard work. Maybe Tammy Jo would give her some reward money or even change her will or something." Then I thought of pretty, pretty Princess Nicki. "But we can't forget Nicki."

I pulled up in front of the Laundry Club and parked. Downtown was empty. Maybe Mayor MacKenzie was right. This murder wasn't good for the community. My stomach dropped at the thought of having to start rebuilding and marketing the campground again if tourists were too scared to come.

"What about her?" Ava didn't like me asking about her.

"When I went to Tammy Jo's to get my check, the front door was cracked open, and I found her on the deck with two wineglasses. One was hers and one was Nicki's." I could see that distinctive orange lipstick right now. "Don't try to convince me Nicki wasn't there to see her mom. Tammy Jo already told me. But why has Nicki come home all of a sudden? When she picked her mom up at the jail, I heard Tammy Jo tell Nicki that she wasn't giving Nicki a dime."

"Oh, dear," Ava sighed. "They don't have the best relationship. Nicki was at the house during the time of the murder, and we were actually going to have a new will reading later that day. That's why she is in town."

"Did Tammy Jo put her in the will?" I asked.

"Not that I should tell you, but Tammy Jo left all her money to Fifi and the long line of breeding that Fifi will leave behind. She's set up an entire committee of people." Ava continued to tell me how she tried to tell Tammy Jo that wasn't a normal thing to do, but my attention was focused on Ethel Biddle as she locked the door of the Smelly Dog. Rosco the pug was attached to a leash that was around Ethel's wrist.

"Listen, Ava. I've got to go, but please get him released. I'll go pick him up, and I'll pay you." I ended the call after she gave a reluctant yes. "Ethel!" I waved and called to her across the street as she started to walk away from the shop.

She waited as I darted across the street, the median, and the other one-way street.

"I wanted to…" I started to say but stopped when Rosco smelled my shoes and let out a few grunts. Bad memories of him rolled around in my head.

"There's no need to thank me. Me and the band love to do little gigs. Keeps me busy." She tugged Rosco a little bit for him to move away from my feet, but he pushed back. His sturdy legs were in a wide stance, and he wasn't budging.

"I wasn't going to say that. I was going to ask you about Fifi." I started to talk again, but she interrupted again.

"I can't help that she flaunted herself in front of my Rosco." Ethel bent down and rubbed Rosco's back. She pulled a treat from her pocket and gave it to him.

"Nope. I wasn't even going to bring that up. I was going to ask you about Fifi's hair appointment. I understand the two of you had an argument about Fifi's tail ball that you cut off." I watched as she slowly stood up. There was a smack of bitterness on her face.

"One minute she wants a puff, the next minute she doesn't. That particular day, she didn't. She went on and on about how the Kentucky Kennel Association was coming to her house, and she wanted Fifi streamlined across the back and up to the tail. The only puffs were on the legs and on her head. *Ahem.*" Ethel cleared her throat and straightened her shoulders while she tightened the leash by rolling it around her hand a couple of times. "As I told Hank Sharp, she left the shop with directions to shave it and her signature on those directions. By the time she got home, she had changed her mind, but I'd already started clipping Fifi. I didn't stop to answer the phone and let my voicemail pick up. When she got there, she went nuts on me and how I didn't know how to listen to the client. I showed her the directions with her signature. She insisted she called me in time to change it, but I didn't even get my messages until that night."

"You already talked to Hank?" I asked.

"Yes, I did. I know it looks bad that we had a public fight, and I knew it was all over town, but like I told Detective Hank, I was clipping another client when Fifi's nanny was murdered. He even took copies of my schedule and my client list with their phone numbers. Now, Rosco and I have an appointment with Norman Pettleman. He's a very busy man, and I can't miss my appointment. Let's go, sweet boy," she said, talking like a baby to the grunting little dog and giving him a gentle tug before he decided to move.

Surely, if Hank had talked to Ethel, he'd already talked to the gardener and Nicki. Well, maybe not with Nicki on a professional level, but by the way he looked at her at the Summer Sizzler party, he was still as smitten with her as Ty Randal. I wanted to gag right there but ran back across the street to get to book club. The girls were going to kill me, and I wasn't ready to join Camille Braun.

Abby Fawn, Betts Hager, Queenie French, and Dottie Swaggert were already sitting at the card table near the bookshelf in the back corner of the Laundry Club. They'd left an open seat for me with a cup of coffee already waiting.

"Just where have you been?" Abby asked. Her hair was pinned up into a bun on the top of her head. She had on her Normal Public Library short-sleeved button-down shirt and a pair of khakis. It was how I knew she'd been working today.

"I had to go to the police station to see Bobby Ray." I glanced over at Dottie. She had the look of "I told you so" on her face. "He didn't do it."

"He had the watch on him." Betts Hager brushed her bangs out of her eyes. "At least, that's what Tammy Jo told Lester."

"Of course, she did. It seems like she's going around telling everyone how innocent she is, but something is fishy. And I can't help but think it's because of her daughter." I gave a direct look to Dottie.

"Listen, I don't know her well enough to even worry with her. She stopped by the campground to say hello because she was in town." Dottie's forehead puckered. "I thought it was strange because she didn't even come to Harrison's funeral. She didn't have use for him since he didn't have the fortune to pay her medical school loans."

"From what I heard, there was a will reading." Queenie cocked her head to the left and rolled her eyes to the right corner of the ceiling. "And I heard our very own Betts and Preacher Hager were invited."

"Listen"—Betts pushed back from the table—"I can't discuss what happens between a member of the church congregation and what business they leave with the church. But it's not unusual for a member to put their church in their will."

"You mean to tell me that you know what the will says?" I licked my lips. This was some news that I needed to get the real killer. "I've got Ava Cox getting Bobby out of jail, because you and I both know"—I gestured between me and Dottie—"he was at the campground when Camille was murdered."

"I can say that Lester is in charge of the scholarships for Fifi's heirs." Betts was trying really hard to pull in the smile that was wanting to form on her lips. "They are going to be taken care of."

"You've got to be kidding me?" Queenie smacked the table, causing us to jump. "That woman is crazy. Maybe whoever killed the dog nanny was really wanting to kill Tammy Jo."

I looked down at my phone when a text chirped in from Ava.

Ava: I got Bobby Ray Bond released. Can't leave town. You're in charge of him. I couldn't take him to Happy Trails. Have to go to Tammy Jo's for a meeting.

Me: Okay. Thank you. I'll get him and be in touch.

I leapt up, my feet hammering across the laundromat floor toward the door.

"Where are you going?" Abby asked.

"I've got to go get Bobby Ray." I pushed open the door of the laundromat and ran across the street. Queenie's suggestion about Tammy Jo being the target was something that I'd let myself forget when I'd initially thought about the murder.

Maybe Camille gave the watch to Bobby Ray as a distraction for something greater. But what?

"Watch where you're going."

I jerked up and nearly tripped over my own feet when a familiar voice interrupted my thoughts.

"Ethel." There was a second of silence while I processed why she'd be standing in front of me on the sidewalk. I looked down at Rosco. He gave a few grunts and snorts. I'm sure it was his way of expressing his disapproval about seeing me again. "I thought you were off to see Norman."

"He had an emergency meeting or something at Tammy Jo's. That Fifi is apparently his number one client." Ethel rolled her eyes. "She's a floozy."

"Fifi?" I asked.

"Mmhhh." Ethel ho-hummed with a contorted face. "She flaunted her pedigree in front of my Rosco."

"Well, it was good seeing you two again." I gave a nod and strode around them to get to my car. "Emergency meeting?" I whispered to myself when I got into the car and wondered exactly what the emergency was. But more importantly, if everyone at Tammy Jo's was in a big meeting, that meant Ralphie, the gardener, just might be alone, and I really wanted to talk to him.

CHAPTER SEVENTEEN

B obby Ray was sitting on the curb outside of the police station. Even though he didn't have a lot of hair, it was still greasy, and a bath was a much-needed event in his future. When I pulled over to pick him up, I noticed Hank's car was parked in the lot.

"May-bell-ine," Bobby Ray gushed when he got into the car. "I don't know how you did it, but I'm so glad you had that lawyer come help me. She was a good one too." He rambled on. "She told that Detective Sharp which way was up and how he didn't even take into consideration my ali-bi." His accent came out in spades. "Where we goin'?" He pointed behind us. "That's the way to the campground."

"I want to see the guest house Camille had you sleep in." I headed out of town toward Tammy Jo's. "And talk to the gardener."

"Why? They let me go." He truly had no idea that letting him leave the jail didn't mean that he wasn't a suspect. "I did ask Camille why the gardener wasn't pulling the weeds, and she said he was busy getting the rest of the grounds ready for the big party they were having."

I knew he was talking about the Kentucky Kennel Association.

"They told you to stay in town and that means you're still on the suspect list. And it means that there's still a killer out there, which means the tourists don't want to come to Normal, which means cancel-

132

lations for Happy Trails. I'm not going back there." It was funny how this was all connected. "Not that I don't want to make sure you're proven innocent, but I haven't worked so hard to let Camille's murder be the thing to bring me down."

"Well, if it's all the same to you, I'm gonna sit in the car because I don't want no part of this." He folded his arms across his chest. His chin jutted out to the side in a defiant sort of way.

It was fine with me. I didn't need the distraction of him while I tried to talk to Ralphie and snoop around a little bit. I wasn't even sure what I was looking for in the guest house, and Hank had probably scoured it, but I had to scratch the itch of my curiosity.

There were many cars at Tammy Jo's. I recognized Ava's and Norman's, but not a couple of the others. Hopefully, they were all so involved in the meeting, they didn't notice me pull up.

"The house is way back there behind that big barn." He pointed out the window.

"I never even noticed that barn back there." It was so far back that I had to squint to even see the top of it. I'd say it was about ten acres away and a good hike from the car. "You stay here. If I'm not back in at least an hour, you come look for me or call Hank." I gave him my phone.

"That makes me think you're worried about something." He looked down at the phone. "Maybe I should go."

"No. I'm fine. I'm sure it'll be good. It's just that there's someone who came here to kill, and they're still not captured. The killer could still be here, and if I'm caught snooping around, they might do to me what they did to Camille." I gulped.

"I think I need to go." He put his hand on the door handle.

"No. You stay here and keep watch." I put my hand on him to stop him because the very last thing I wanted was to be babysitting Bobby Ray when I could slip in and out of there practically unseen.

"Alright. One hour." He gave a good hard nod.

My best course of action was to not be seen. Taking the way around the tree line toward the barn to do that might've been a little longer walk, but it was shaded and kept me out of the glaring hot sun and sight of the house.

The shade sounded like a great idea, but the humidity crept up on my skin, giving me a sweaty glow that even the shadow of the trees couldn't help. I scrambled as quickly as I could across the ten acres until I reached the small guesthouse Bobby Ray had said was there.

I took a look around to make sure everything was clear before I decided to turn the doorknob. There was a clear view of the back of the house from here, and the tents that were on the lawn for the party were long gone.

I squeezed the door handle, and somehow, I convinced myself that if the door was open, it wouldn't necessarily be breaking and entering if I got caught... uninvited.

As if it were meant to be, my hand curled around the knob, and it turned. The air conditioner whipped out cold air that flooded over me. Then, time slowed almost to a standstill. My heartbeat pounded, the veins in my forehead pumped with the beat, and my entire body began to shake at the sight of Ralphie, lying on the floor just behind the door with blood oozing out of his chest.

"No!" I screamed as loud as I could. I couldn't tell you really what happened next or how things progressed because the only thing that snapped me out of the hell I was in was Nicki Swaggert, who came running in behind me.

Of all people.

"Mae," she called my name, shaking me back into my right mind. "Let's get you out of here." She had a hand on each of my shoulders. She tried to shift me right. My feet didn't move. My eyes focused on the poor gardener. Nicki's grip shifted me left. Again, my feet and eyes didn't move.

"Call Hank" was all I could get out of my mouth.

"I think we need to get you out of here first." She squeezed even harder.

Under normal circumstances, I'd have felt the pain of her fingernails as they pressed into my skin, but I was numb. Nothing seemed to be working.

"Are you okay, May-bell-ine?" I heard Bobby Ray huffing and puffing, running up to us. My mouth opened, and nothing came out. My mouth closed. "Camille? I thought you were dead." His words brought me right out of my shock, causing me to jerk from her grip.

"Camille?" I twirled around. "This isn't Camille. This is Nicki Swaggert."

I remembered Camille's face when we were standing in front of the mantle and the dome-covered watch when she looked at the dirt spot on the carpet. She really didn't know how the stain got there, and it was Bobby Ray's.

"Did you pretend to be Camille?" My heart started to race, my palms began to sweat, and goosebumps crawled up my arms.

"Now, May-bell-ine." Bobby Ray's eyes dragged past my shoulder, and he looked at Ralphie. "Let's me and you get on out of here and leave Camille alone."

"Bobby," I gasped, "this isn't Camille." Like a puzzle, I saw all the pieces coming together. "You!" I pointed to her. "Bobby Ray, use my phone to call the police. Now!"

"I didn't do anything. You just stop right there." She pointed her fancy manicured finger at Bobby. "I never told you I was Camille."

"But you gave me the watch, and the paper said you were dead." Bobby's brows furrowed. He looked all sorts of confused.

"Call the police with my phone. Call 911," I instructed him.

"Let's just all go back to the house, and we can get this all straightened out." Nicki tried to come across slick but sounded a little anxious.

All I could do was shiver and shake in my shoes.

"Nah"—Bobby Ray's nose curled—"I think May-bell-ine might be right. We should just call the police here."

Another familiar voice came from behind us. "Yeah. I don't think so. I'm going to have to ask you to take a seat on the couch over there."

Norman Pettleman was standing behind us with a gun that I could only assume was the same gun used to kill Ralphie. A blanket of fear choked out the cool air from the air conditioner. Even Nicki Swaggert seemed to be shaking and nervous.

"Norman?" Nicki's voice cracked.

"I'm sure you're a nice girl, but after all of this, you're going to be the one going to jail for killing him, him, and her." He pointed his gun at Ralphie, Bobby Ray, and me.

"I'm sorry, Nicki. I thought you were the one who wanted your mother's money, but all this time, it was Norman." The last piece of the puzzle was fitting into place.

"Nicki here thought she was being sneaky when she took the watch and gave it to Hillbilly Bobby over here." Norman pointed the gun at Bobby and snickered at his cleverness.

There was fire in Bobby's eyes that I'd not seen since the day he beat up a kid in high school who called Bobby Ray a hillbilly.

"What? I hurt your feelings?" Norman snorted, and the gun twitched. It was then that I knew Norman felt just as much anxiety as we were feeling.

"Norman, take the watch. I don't want it." Nicki said. She and Norman began to have a conversation as I continued to put the last of this insane puzzle together.

"You thought you'd come back in here and just get all the money, when I'm the one who put up with that stupid dog. The entire insurance community is talking about what an idiot I am for insuring the cloning of a dog. Well, I'm not so stupid. Your mother is about to make me the beneficiary now that poor Camille is dead." Norman kept the gun pointed at me as he slowly walked over to Nicki, pulling her by her arm and lifting her off the couch. "Get over to the kitchen table, and I want you to write a note."

Norman exhaled a frustration of impatience and pushed Nicki forward.

"I don't have time for all of this. Hurry up." His eyes darted between everyone in the room. "I want you to write, 'Dear mother,'" he said. "I'm sorry. I really wanted to be back in your life, but the jealousy about you loving a dog more than me is just too much for me to take. I couldn't stand the sight of Camille and how much you trusted her. Out of rage, I had to get rid of her and gave the watch to that low-life drifter. When I picked you up from jail and his alibi cleared, I came home only to find Ralphie. He was going to blackmail me because he'd seen me run from dad's office that morning."

Norman thought he was so brilliant. He made his letter sound so dramatic like something you'd see in a movie. All the shows I'd been watching made this look fishy, but I kept my mouth shut and looked around to find a way to get out of this.

Bobby didn't move. His hands were fisted in tight balls on his thighs, his back was straight, his jaw was tense, and his eyes didn't move off of Norman, even when I tried to get his attention by sliding my foot over to nudge his.

"Unfortunately, Mae West couldn't keep her nose out of my business or control her jealousy about how much Hank and Ty are still in love with me and not her." Norman stopped talking and looked at me, an evil grin on his face.

My eyelids lowered. There were so many emotions bubbling up inside of me.

"What?" He grunted my way. "You don't think I didn't notice those two men fawning over you these past few months? It just makes it real convenient that the two of you have something in common."

He turned back to Nicki.

"Write." He poked her with the gun in her arm. She winced and let out a little cry. "Mae had to die too. The hillbilly, well, no one is going to miss him."

"You're telling me that you killed Camille because my mom didn't name you as the beneficiary on the insurance?" All of a sudden Nicki found her voice.

"You're telling me that you stole the watch because you knew your mom would handsomely reward you if you were the one to find it, and you were willing to throw this hillbilly under the bus?" Norman mocked her.

Then it was clear. The puzzle was complete. There were two crimes here. Both of them trying to scam Tammy Jo out of her money.

"You two weren't working together?" I suddenly couldn't move or think when Norman rushed over, sticking the gun in my face.

"You're smarter than I thought." His eyes grew big and scary, like Jack Nicholson in *The Shining*.

"Here's Bobby!" Bobby jumped up, knocking the gun out of Norman's hand.

Nicki and I both lunged to grab the gun after it hit the wall, landing on the floor.

"Yes!" I screamed in delight when my hand grabbed the barrel of the gun, jerking it from Nicki. "Now it's my turn."

I held the gun on Nicki, then pointed it toward Norman. "Call 911," I instructed Bobby Ray, who was now sitting on top of Norman Pettleman, nearly squishing the life out of him. I dragged my phone out of my back pocket and tossed it to him.

"You're going down. Both of you," I said.

"No one calls me a hillbilly." Bobby bounced a little on top of Norman. "There's been a murder at Tammy Jo Bentley's guesthouse, and the killer is currently being detained," Bobby said into the phone.

CHAPTER EIGHTEEN

"You mean to tell me that Nicki came to town to steal the watch, which she had Bobby Ray hold until she came looking for it?" Dottie asked from her desk in the campground office.

Both of us were pretty pleased with the reservations at the campground. The season was changing to fall, which happened to be my favorite season in Kentucky. As a child, I remembered how the green leaves made a beautiful painting across the state as they changed to red, orange, and yellow. I'd yet to be at Happy Trails in the fall, and I could only imagine what the Daniel Boone National Forest looked like. It was something I was looking forward to.

Dottie handed me the final reservation to put into the computer.

"Yes. Can you believe it? Bobby Ray was just at the right spot at the right time." I typed away as fast as I could. I'd been waiting for tonight for a long time, and I needed to get out of here to get ready. "Norman and Camille were actually an item."

It'd come out that Camille had stopped seeing Ralphie because of Norman. Norman had used his slick salesman skills to talk Camille into convincing Tammy Jo to make her the beneficiary of the insurance policy. When Camille started to get nervous about it, she was going to come clean to Tammy Jo about Norman's plan because Camille had really grown to love and care for Fifi and Tammy Jo.

"After Camille was found dead, Ralphie went to Norman and told Norman that he knew his little scheme. The day I was there to clean, Norman was there to try and get Tammy Jo to make him the beneficiary. He tried to claim he got better coverage since he was the owner of the insurance agency." I hit the send button on the computer, which sent the reservation to the calendar on the website, showing those days were booked. "Norman wasn't about to let Ralphie ruin his chances, so Ralphie became an unfortunate victim."

"Let me get this straight, even with Nicki hiding the watch, the insurance would cover it? Either way, Norman would benefit from it." I could see the wheels in Dottie's head churning as she tried to put the pieces together.

"Yeah. Nicki was always planning on giving the watch back. She'd planted one of those Tracfones in Bobby's backpack. She'd put a fake text on there like it was from him saying he'd scored the watch." It seemed so unreal to me that Nicki thought this was going to work.

"Now I feel bad I was so mean to Bobby Ray." Dottie's feelings for Bobby were changing and that made me happy since he didn't appear to be leaving anytime soon.

"Yeah. She thought he was really just a hiker that no one would ever find. She planned on meeting him to get the watch back and letting him go on his way. She told Hank she was going to say that she confronted him, and he took off, dropping the watch behind him," I said, explaining to Dottie what I'd overheard after Hank had made it to the crime scene.

"That's just crazy." Dottie rubbed her head. "Harrison always said Nicki only loved him because of the money he gave her. When he and Tammy got divorced, Nicki never came around him. Even on his deathbed."

"Nicki only wanted to be in good graces with Tammy Jo so she could get in on some inheritance. She has so many loans from medical school; she's drowning in debt. Norman just wanted to scam her to get rich. Two different crimes that Hank Sharp is going to have to figure out."

Dottie and I looked at the office door when it jerked open.

"Tammy Jo," I greeted her and pushed the off button on the computer monitor. "Fifi." My voice escalated when I saw the fluffy white poodle squirm out of Tammy Jo's arms and bounce over to me. I bent down and picked her up. "I've missed you."

Fifi's rear end wiggled with joy as she licked my face.

"Here you go." Tammy Jo trotted in and dropped Fifi's pink bag on my desk. "She's all yours."

"All mine?" I asked with an uneasy feeling.

"Yep. You let her wander on the wrong side of the tracks. Now her problem is your problem." Tammy Jo's frustration was rising with each word.

"What are you talking about?" I was all sorts of confused.

"Rosco? She's pregnant." The lines on her forehead creased as her scowl at me deepened. "I can't insure her now that you've ruined her. So, she's all yours. Besides..." Her features hardened. "She's not been eating since she came home. I think she missed you."

"No." I held Fifi out at arm's length. "I don't have time for a dog."

"What about her offspring and your insurance on cloning her?" It was strange to me that she'd spend these past four years grooming a dog and taking the time to get all the paperwork, insurance, and place in the KKA, just to give Fifi to me.

"I'm going to cash it in and take a much-needed vacation far away from Normal. Like I said, she's your problem now." Tammy Jo twirled around on the balls of her feet and didn't even look back on her way out the door.

Dottie Swaggert was bent over, laughing herself silly.

"I'm glad you think this is funny." I put Fifi on the ground, and she sat down, looking up at me with those big, round black eyes. I swear she was smiling. "What am I going to do with a dog?"

"Whatever she wants." Dottie snorted.

"What am I going to do with her tonight?" I looked up at the clock on the wall. I had to get going. "I've been waiting for my date with Ty for what seems like forever."

"I guess his boys are going to watch her for you." Dottie grabbed her keys off her desk. "I'm going home for the night. I'll see you two in the morning."

"I hope you know you're taking a puppy!" I yelled at Dottie on her way out of the office.

Fifi stood up and let out a little yip before she did a couple of circles.

"If you're going to be living here, you're going to be dirty and tired and have no leash." I unclipped the harness from around her and stuck it in the bag. "No more vitamins or fancy food." I spoke to her like she understood me.

She yipped a few more times.

"Fine." I swept the bag into the garbage can and flipped the light off on our way out.

It was like she understood everything I said because she darted ahead of me toward the camper. It was a pleasant surprise that she was waiting for me on the steps of the camper like she knew it was her home.

"You are smart." I couldn't help but smile at her little white paws knowing it was going to kill me to try to keep her clean.

I opened the door to the camper, and she darted in like she owned the place. Down in my heart, it did feel like she belonged. I'd never admit that the past couple of nights since she'd been back with Tammy Jo, I was a little sad. It was lonely and for a second—only a second—I'd thought about going to visit the local animal shelter to pick out a dog. I'd never imagined it'd be a poodle, much less Fifi.

"I've got a very important date tonight," I told her, but she'd already curled up on the blanket on the couch. "I think you're going to fit in just fine here."

I walked over to her and ran my finger over her belly. She lifted her head and looked at me, blinking those cute eyes. There was a moment between us, and my heart fluttered.

"You rest, little mama." It was then and there that I realized I'd not been alone this entire time I'd been in Normal. I'd spent the better part of my time here trying to take care of everyone around me, and now, I had a sweet dog to take care of. "I've got a dinner date with Ty Randal."

I had just enough time to get in a shower and slip into a little black dress that I'd kept from my past, along with the perfect pair of strappy sandals. My face was slightly tan from the last days of summer, which let me use minimal makeup. I swiped some bright-red lipstick on and flat ironed my hair just in time for my date to arrive.

"I can't wait to see where you're taking me." I flung the door open. "I'm starving."

"Wow." Hank Sharp was standing outside with a bouquet of flowers in his hand. "You look great, Mae."

"Hank?" I was startled to see him here. "What are you doing here?"

"I stopped by for some cahoots." He grinned, holding the flowers out to me.

My heart sank into my stomach. I glanced over his shoulder, and Ty Randal stood behind him about ten feet away.

Hank looked at me and turned around.

"Ty." Hank took a step back. "Did I interrupt something?"

"Mae," Ty said and walked up. "I think Timmy is getting sick. He's got a fever, and I've not gone to the grocery yet."

By the way he was talking, I knew our dinner date was going to have to wait some more.

"What can I do?" I asked.

"I wanted to know if you had any Tylenol?" he asked and smiled. His face softened, and I smiled back.

"Yes. Let me get it." I shut the door to get the medicine.

I pulled the curtain over the kitchen sink back just enough for me to see out. The two men were standing there, silence between them.

I opened the door and walked down the two steps to give the medicine to Ty.

"Here you go. Keep it. Please let me know if I can do anything else." Our fingers touched, and we looked at each other at the same time. "Maybe another night."

"Definitely," Ty said before he turned back to go and take care of his little brother.

The sun was setting a little earlier than normal, which was signaling the end of summer. Soon it would be dark, and all the campfires would be lit. The smell of food, wood, and the outdoors would blanket the campground.

"Are those for me?" I asked Hank to break the uncomfortable silence between us.

"Yes. I'm sorry. I really feel like I've interrupted something." He handed me the flowers. "I mean, you look like you're going out."

"Nah." I tipped my head toward the camper. "Come in. I've got something to show you."

If anyone would get a kick out of what Tammy Jo Bentley had given me, Hank Sharp would.

He followed me up the steps. While he saw my surprise inside, I looked toward Ty's camper before I shut the door. He'd stopped before he went inside his camper. I wasn't sure if it was one of the last lightning bugs of the season or if it was a twinkle in Ty's eye, but I'd like to think it was the latter.

"Mae?" Hank called to me from inside.

"Coming." I shut the camper door behind me.

THE END

If you enjoyed reading this book as much as I enjoyed writing it then be sure to return to the Amazon page and leave a review.

Go to Tonyakappes.com for a full reading order of my novels and while there join my newsletter. You can also find links to Facebook, Instagram and Goodreads.

Keep reading for a sneak peek of Book Three Forests, Fishing, & Forgery

Chapter One of Book Three
Forests, Fishing, & Forgery

"Welcome to Happy Trails Campground and to our party." If I'd said it once, I'd said it a million times today. "Here is our brochure. We cater to campers with tents, pop-ups, fifth wheels, and vans." I smiled and shrugged. "We cater to all. Even the ones who need a place to sleep." I flipped open the brochure to show the young couple who'd come to the monthly party we hosted. "We have cute bungalows that range in size and need. Are you here for the long Labor Day weekend?"

"We've been wanting to do the whole Appalachian Trail but figured we'd better do some smaller hiking first." There was an eager look on the young woman's face that I'd seen before. "We have a couple of days off and thought we'd drive down and check it all out."

"I'm the hiker. Beth here, well…" The young man's eyes squinted as he smiled at her. "She's more along the lines of a glamper."

"Oh, silly." Beth rolled her eyes and put her hand on his chest. "Chuck doesn't give me much credit. Don't get me wrong. I love room service and a good spa, but if we are going to get married, I'd better start doing something he likes."

"Then Happy Trails is for you." I looked between them. "The Appalachian Plateau goes right through the Daniel Boone National Forest." I pointed toward the lake. "I know you can't see it now because of all the people gathered around the band, but right beyond the tree line is the start of a beautiful five-mile hike. It's maybe one step above a beginner, but it will bring you to an amazing waterfall."

"Beth?" Chuck put his hands out. "It's up to you. A bungalow or the bed and breakfast downtown?"

The door of the office swung open. Dottie Swaggert's unlit cigarette bounced between her dry lips. She pushed her hands up in her short red hair, fluffing it out a little.

"I'm sorry to bother you, Mae. Someone's on the phone about the last bungalow for rent. I told them the fee, and they insisted on talking to the owner." Her brows cocked. "I told them that you was busy with the party, but they insisted and if I know you…" She looked between Chuck and Beth. "Trust me, I know her. You'd want me to come get you."

Dottie held the portable phone.

"You only have one bungalow left for rent?" Chuck asked, his brows knitted together with worry.

"I do. We were totally booked, but due to some unforeseen circumstances, someone cancelled at the last minute." I took a few steps closer to Dottie to get the phone. "Thanks to social media and all those hashtags, we usually fill a vacancy within minutes of a cancellation."

It was true. For years, I'd said I'd never get on social media. That was before I became the owner of Happy Trails Campground in Normal, Kentucky, sight unseen. Once I did see it… boy howdy. It'd needed a redo more than I needed a life do-over. That was why Happy Trails and I were perfect for each other. I had discovered not only myself but that social media could help a business better than any other type of marketing.

Just as I extended my arm to grab the phone, Beth began to stutter and mumble something.

"What?" I asked and leaned in an ear.

"We'll take it." Beth bounced on her toes and clasped her hands together. She looked at Chuck. "Right?" The tone in her voice didn't seem so sure.

"Right!" Chuck jumped at the chance. Beth threw her arms around Chuck.

"Dottie, can you please tell the person on the phone the bungalow is no longer available?" I asked her, knowing that she'd set this whole thing up. It wasn't the first time someone was on the fence about renting either a lot or a bungalow and Dottie pulled the old someone-wants-to-rent-now trick, making it a tad more urgent for Chuck and Beth to say yes.

All of us turned around when we heard quick toots of a car horn followed by a couple of long beeps from a fast-paced carload of people driving up from the entrance of the campground.

"Woo-hoo!" said a young man with a big smile, dangling his arm out the window. There was a beer in the grip of his hand and a flashy watch on his wrist. The car came to an abrupt stop.

I sucked in a deep breath and let out a slight moan. This wasn't the impression I wanted Beth and Chuck to have on their first camping experience.

"Guys, settle down," said the driver, who was also a young man, as the others started to celebrate their arrival and he tried to calm them down. He got out of the car and stuck his head back through the driver's side window to give the group one last scolding.

"Why don't we go ahead and get you registered?" I gestured for Beth and Chuck to follow me into the office. I glanced at Dottie. "Why don't you see what they want?" I suggested, knowing she didn't take a whole lot of bull and would send them on their way.

"I'll be more than happy to do that." The look of satisfaction on her face made me smile.

"Sorry about that." I wanted to make sure Chuck and Beth knew Happy Trails was a nice, relaxing place with fun, not rowdy, guests. There was an immediate need for me to apologize.

The office space wasn't big. It was just a small, open space with metal files and two desks. There was a big window on each wall, which made it easy for us to see all sides of the campground while we were in there.

"Here are some papers I need you to fill out." I handed them a clipboard with all the papers and a pen tied around the metal clip with a piece of yarn. "This one is for the rental agreement. It has all the particulars about trash and how you need to leave things after you check out." I flipped through each page as I pointed out what they were. "I'll need a copy of your license for safety purposes if you are going to be hiking. Not that we've lost a hiker," I assured them.

My eyes glanced over their shoulders, and I could see that the car of boys had emptied out. All of them were standing with their arms crossed, arguing with Dottie.

"While you fill those out, I'm going to go check on Dottie." I didn't want those boys to bring any undue attention to the campground, especially since they were here during our monthly themed party. I shut the door behind me. "Is everything okay out here?"

"I want to see the owner, and she won't let us," the one I recognized as the driver told me. "I've had a reservation for me and my friends for months. It's my bachelor weekend."

"They don't have their reservation number." Dottie's eyes lowered. She wasn't too trusting of people, and it made her a great office manager.

"William Hinson." I stuck my arm out for him to shake.

"Yes, that's me," he said in a calm voice and straightened his shoulders a little more. "Do you have our reservation?"

"I do. Remember the reservation that was booked for two weeks because we don't do middle-of-the-week reservations for the bungalows?" I looked over at Dottie. Whoever had booked the bachelor party had reserved the bungalow way in advance. "Your bride sent a few items for you and your friends ahead of time."

A couple of days ago, we'd gotten a big package in the mail from William's bride-to-be. It was filled with snacks, movies, and gear for hiking and fishing.

"She did?" He grinned.

The other four boys patted his back.

"He's got a good one."

I recognized the one that was flailing his arm out the car window earlier.

"Jamison." He nodded at me. "My name is Jamison Todd Downey."

"I get that. I'm Mae." I wasn't about to give my full name, which was Maybelline Grant West. It wasn't uncommon for Southerners to give you their full names upon introduction. The more we talked, the less rowdy they were, just excited.

"You've got these yahoos?" Dottie wasn't very forgiving when a first impression made her cringe. I could feel the tension coming off her shoulders as they hugged her ears.

"I will take them to their bungalow while you finish up with Beth and Chuck," I said to Dottie.

It was nice to be able to team up with Dottie. She'd been the manager at Happy Trails way before I'd gotten there. I'd come to rely on her for a lot of things, but hospitality to everyone wasn't her specialty. She was fabulous at putting together parties and keeping the campground running like a well-oiled machine, but she didn't take any nonsense, which these boys seemed to have plenty of.

"Hold on a second," I told the boys and went back into the office with Dottie. "Beth and Chuck, this is Dottie. She's going to finish up getting y'all settled. You're in great hands."

They nodded eagerly and went back to filling out the paperwork. I walked over to the filing cabinet and opened the *H* drawer for Hinson to find William's reservation. There was a lot of paperwork and computer work to be done. It was best to get him to fill out the paper-work at the bungalow he'd rented instead of bringing him into the office with the couple.

"They might need a starter camping kit," I said to Dottie about the couple. I grabbed the key to the bungalow with four bedrooms where we'd stuck William and his friends, plus a clipboard full of paperwork. "I'm not sure if they've got towels and things either."

When I finally got settled into being the owner of Happy Trails, I realized many campers forget everyday things like toothbrushes, towels, and other personal hygiene items. That was when I came up with the idea to put together camper packs. We offered them at several different prices, depending on what was included. We also rented fishing and hiking supplies, including poles, backpacks, and picnic baskets.

I partnered with a few of the local shops in Normal, offering their items in different baskets. The Cookie Crumble Bakery's delicious chocolate chip cookies that were the size of my head were a hit, along with coffee from the new coffeehouse in town.

Gert Hobson, owner of the Trails Coffee Shop, put together packages of coffee and filters for the rental campers and the bungalows. She also supplied the complimentary coffee I offered in the morning at the recreation center on the campground. Anytime I could help a local store, I did.

"Are you good?" I asked Dottie before I left to get the boys settled into their bungalow. I could see there was still some tension about the Hinson bachelor party.

"I'm fine." She didn't sound fine, but there wasn't any way to question her in front of customers, so I left and decided I'd take it up with her later.

"Why don't you head on down to bungalow five? I'll be right behind you." I put the items in the golf cart. The bungalows were located at the farthest end of the campground and were more nestled into the woods while the concrete pads for the campers were out in the open, with a few lots that had tree coverage.

"Thank you." William took the keys. "Boys, back in the car." He lifted his arm in the air and twirled his finger around. They all piled in.

"Y'all sure do have some fancy watches." I noticed they all looked alike too.

"I got them for all the groomsmen as their present for being in my wedding. They even have their initials engraved on the back." He flipped his off and showed me.

Southerners loved to put their initials on everything. Including shower curtains.

"Be sure you adhere to the fifteen-mile-an-hour speed limit," I warned him. That was something I'd definitely kick them out of the campground for. We had many families with children and pets, including my Fifi. "I'll be right behind you. First, I have to stop by my own camper."

They took off in their car, and I got into the golf cart. Fall in Love with Kentucky was the theme of the month and honored Labor Day. Dottie loved how she incorporated the fall season in the name. It was one of the most popular seasons at the Daniel Boone National Forest.

She'd used different camping items to decorate: canoes, a couple of tents decorated with bobbers and plastic fish, checkered tablecloths, bourbon barrels, and campfires going with a s'more station.

The recreation center had games for everyone, including cornhole, horseshoes, and ladder golf, just to name a few. Blue Ethel and the Adolescent Farm Boys were on the stage singing their hearts out while they played the banjo, guitar, harmonica, and jug. It was a true bluegrass band that went nicely with the theme.

There were cornstalks and bales of hay all over the place for extra seating. Pumpkins, gourds, and colorful mums filled old tobacco baskets and planters of different sizes.

I pushed down the gas pedal on the golf cart to head on down to my camper. The fresh air filled my lungs and spread a happiness through my body. A few months ago, I'd never imagined myself here, much less the owner. When I found out I was the owner, I'd decided I was going to sell it as fast as I could find a buyer. As I started to get to know the small, southern town of Normal, the more I began to enjoy the slow-paced life surrounded by nature. It was food for the soul, and when a buyer did come along, there was no way I could even imagine letting it go. Dottie Swaggert and I, along with many members of the community, had brought Happy Trails back to what it used to be.

For me... it was home.

Forests, Fishing, & Forgery is now available to purchase or in Kindle Unlimited.

RECIPES AND CLEANING HACKS FROM MAE WEST AND THE
LAUNDRY CLUB LADIES AT THE HAPPY TRAILS CAMPGROUND
IN NORMAL KENTUCKY.

Bobby Ray Bond's Campfire Pigs in a Blanket

Ingredients

- 1 can crescent roll dough
- 2 tbsp. mustard
- 8 hot dogs
- 8 skewers

Directions

Separate crescent dough into triangles. Spread a very thin layer of mustard over each piece of dough then place a hot dog on top. Roll up, so the dough is wrapped around the hot dog, then insert a skewer into each dog.

Cook over a campfire until the crescent is golden and the dough is cooked through, 10 to 15 minutes.

Campfire Waffles and Peanut Butter Cones

Ingredients

- 6 waffle cones
- Mini marshmallows
- Reese's Peanut Butter Cup Miniatures
- Reese's Pieces
- Peanut butter

Directions

1. Stuff cones with marshmallows, Reese's Peanut Butter Cups, Reese's Pieces, and peanut butter.
2. Wrap cones with foil and throw on the campfire until the candies are melted, about 5 minutes.
3. Remove from heat and let rest until cool enough to handle.

Foil Breakfast Pack

Ingredients

- 6 large eggs
- 1/2 c. milk
- Kosher salt
- Freshly ground black pepper
- 1 lb. refrigerated hash browns (thawed, if frozen)
- 1 c. chopped ham
- 2 c. shredded cheddar
- Butter, for foil
- Chopped fresh chives, for garnish

Directions

1. In a large resealable plastic bag, crack eggs, add milk, and season with salt and pepper. Stir in hash browns, ham, and cheese.
2. Butter four squares of aluminum foil and divide mixture among the pieces of foil. Fold tightly and seal.
3. Place packets over campfire or grill and cook until eggs are cooked, and hash browns are tender and crispy, about 10 minutes.
4. Garnish with chives and serve.

Cleaning Hack
Get Rid of Rust Spots

If you notice spots of rust forming on your silverware, there is a simple solution! Soak your stained silverware in a glass of lemon juice and then rinse them off before drying. As you hand dry them, the rust stains should magically wipe away!

Tortilla Chip Fire Starters

Got a bunch of wood but can't get it lit? Try using some tortilla chips to get it going. They burn like crazy and can help you get a roaring fire going in no time. This will actually work with most fried chips, as it is the oils in the chips that are flammable. Doritos and Fritos seem to work especially well.

Sage as Mosquito Repellent

One of my favorite things about camping in the American West is the smell of sage. Sometimes, on long white-water rafting trips, I will tuck a small sprig of sage into my life jacket strap so I can smell the fresh desert perfume as I float down the river. But sage also has some practical uses, and one of them is as a mosquito repellent. Just pick a few small branches and toss them in the campfire to help keep the mosquitoes from bothering you. Now you can relax and enjoy the fire instead of spending the night swatting at those pesky little bloodsuckers.

A NOTE FROM TONYA

Thank y'all so much for this amazing journey we've been on with all the fun cozy mystery adventures! We've had so much fun and I can't wait to bring you a lot more of them. When I set out to write about them, I pulled from my experiences from camping, having a camper, and fond memories of camping.

Readers ask me if there's a real place like those in my books. Sadly, no. It's a combination of places I've stayed and would own if I could.
 XOXO ~ Tonya

For a full reading order of Tonya Kappes's Novels, visit
Tonyakappes.com

BOOKS BY TONYA
SOUTHERN HOSPITALITY WITH A SMIDGEN OF HOMICIDE

Camper & Criminals Cozy Mystery Series

All is good in the camper-hood until a dead body shows up in the woods.

BEACHES, BUNGALOWS, AND BURGLARIES
DESERTS, DRIVING, & DERELICTS
FORESTS, FISHING, & FORGERY
CHRISTMAS, CRIMINALS, AND CAMPERS
MOTORHOMES, MAPS, & MURDER
CANYONS, CARAVANS, & CADAVERS
HITCHES, HIDEOUTS, & HOMICIDES
ASSAILANTS, ASPHALT & ALIBIS
VALLEYS, VEHICLES & VICTIMS
SUNSETS, SABBATICAL AND SCANDAL
TENTS, TRAILS AND TURMOIL
KICKBACKS, KAYAKS, AND KIDNAPPING
GEAR, GRILLS & GUNS
EGGNOG, EXTORTION, AND EVERGREEN
ROPES, RIDDLES, & ROBBERIES
PADDLERS, PROMISES & POISON
INSECTS, IVY, & INVESTIGATIONS
OUTDOORS, OARS, & OATH
WILDLIFE, WARRANTS, & WEAPONS
BLOSSOMS, BBQ, & BLACKMAIL
LANTERNS, LAKES, & LARCENY
JACKETS, JACK-O-LANTERN, & JUSTICE
SANTA, SUNRISES, & SUSPICIONS
VISTAS, VICES, & VALENTINES
ADVENTURE, ABDUCTION, & ARREST

RANGERS, RVS, & REVENGE
CAMPFIRES, COURAGE & CONVICTS
TRAPPING, TURKEY & THANKSGIVING
GIFTS, GLAMPING & GLOCKS
ZONING, ZEALOTS, & ZIPLINES
HAMMOCKS, HANDGUNS, & HEARSAY
QUESTIONS, QUARRELS, & QUANDARY
WITNESS, WOODS, & WEDDING
ELVES, EVERGREENS, & EVIDENCE
MOONLIGHT, MARSHMALLOWS, & MANSLAUGHTER
BONFIRE, BACKPACKS, & BRAWLS

Killer Coffee Cozy Mystery Series

Welcome to the Bean Hive Coffee Shop where the gossip is just as hot as the coffee.

SCENE OF THE GRIND
MOCHA AND MURDER
FRESHLY GROUND MURDER
COLD BLOODED BREW
DECAFFEINATED SCANDAL
A KILLER LATTE
HOLIDAY ROAST MORTEM
DEAD TO THE LAST DROP
A CHARMING BLEND NOVELLA (CROSSOVER WITH MAGICAL CURES MYSTERY)
FROTHY FOUL PLAY
SPOONFUL OF MURDER
BARISTA BUMP-OFF
CAPPUCCINO CRIMINAL
MACCHIATO MURDER
POUR-OVER PREDICAMENT
ICE COFFEE CORRUPTION

Holiday Cozy Mystery Series

CELEBRATE GOOD CRIMES!

FOUR LEAF FELONY
MOTHER'S DAY MURDER
A HALLOWEEN HOMICIDE
NEW YEAR NUISANCE
CHOCOLATE BUNNY BETRAYAL
FOURTH OF JULY FORGERY
SANTA CLAUSE SURPRISE
APRIL FOOL'S ALIBI

Kenni Lowry Mystery Series

*Mysteries so delicious it'll make your mouth water and leave you
hankerin' for more.*

FIXIN' TO DIE
SOUTHERN FRIED
AX TO GRIND
SIX FEET UNDER
DEAD AS A DOORNAIL
TANGLED UP IN TINSEL
DIGGIN' UP DIRT
BLOWIN' UP A MURDER
HEAVENS TO BRIBERY

Magical Cures Mystery Series

Welcome to Whispering Falls where magic and mystery collide.

A CHARMING CRIME
A CHARMING CURE

TANGLED LIES
GRAVE DECEPTION

About Tonya

Tonya has written over 100 novels, all of which have graced numerous bestseller lists, including the USA Today. *Best known for stories charged with emotion and humor and filled with flawed characters, her novels have garnered reader praise and glowing critical reviews. She lives with her husband and a very spoiled rescue cat named Ro. Tonya grew up in the small southern Kentucky town of Nicholasville. Now that her four boys are grown men, Tonya writes full-time in her camper she calls her SHAMPER (she-camper).*

Learn more about her be sure to check out her website tonyakappes.com. Find her on Facebook, Twitter, BookBub, and Instagram

Sign up to receive her newsletter, where you'll get free books, exclusive bonus content, and news of her releases and sales.

If you liked this book, please take a few minutes to leave a review now! Authors (Tonya included) really appreciate this, and it helps draw more readers to books they might like. Thanks!